A Candlelight Ecstasy Romance ®

MIKE CAUGHT HOLD OF HER ARM AND SWUNG HER AROUND.

"I know damn well you're not a twenty-seven-year-old virgin. So who does get between those sheets with you if it isn't a model or one of your socialite beaus?"

Stacy slapped him with all her strength. Mike pushed her hard against the sink. Then, the next minute, he was pressing against her, his mouth descending, capturing hers with a fierce possessiveness.

"Sorry, Stacy, I guess I can be as ridiculous, unreasonable, and jealous as you."

She gave him a long, hard look before her features softened into a hint of a smile. She was also aware that, although Mike had loosened his steely grip, his arms still held her lightly.

"You do have a maddening effect on me," he said, drawing a deep breath. "I keep forgetting all our vows to behave. How about you?"

When he bent his head toward her this time, Stacy's face was already tilted up to meet him.

CANDLELIGHT ECSTASY ROMANCES®

TOO GOOD TO BE TRUE

Alison Tyler

A CANDLELIGHT ECSTASY ROMANCE ®

Published by
Dell Publishing Co., Inc.
1 Dag Hammarskjold Plaza
New York, New York 10017

Dell ® TM 681510, Dell Publishing Co., Inc.
Candlelight Ecstasy Romance®, 1,203,540, is a registered
trademark of Dell Publishing Co., Inc.,
New York, New York.

ISBN: 0-440-19006-1

Printed in the United States of America
First printing—June 1984

To Our Readers:

We have been delighted with your enthusiastic response to Candlelight Ecstasy Romances®, and we thank you for the interest you have shown in this exciting series.

In the upcoming months we will continue to present the distinctive sensuous love stories you have come to expect only from Ecstasy. We look forward to bringing you many more books from your favorite authors and also the very finest work from new authors of contemporary romantic fiction.

As always, we are striving to present the unique, absorbing love stories that you enjoy most—books that are more than ordinary romance.

Your suggestions and comments are always welcome. Please write to us at the address below.

Sincerely,

The Editors
Candlelight Romances
1 Dag Hammarskjold Plaza
New York, New York 10017

CHAPTER ONE

Stacy English couldn't find her coffee mug. It could be anywhere amidst the disarray of her large SoHo loft. Abandoning the search with a shrug, she poured a fresh cup. Sipping the strong brew, Stacy double-checked her appointment pad. She was eager to get going.

There was a firm rap on the door. Forgetting that she was still holding the mug of coffee, Stacy flicked her wrist to check the time. The black liquid, luckily lukewarm at this point with the cup only half-full, splashed all over her dungarees in the process. Silently cursing, she watched the almost white splotches of dried clay that decorated her jeans turn a dark murky gray. The action was so ridiculously slapstick, she couldn't help laughing despite her annoyance. Still chuckling, she shouted, "Come in."

Scooting across the room for a sheet of toweling to sop up the moisture, Stacy was busy blotting her dungarees as the door opened.

"Miss English?" The voice was deep, a touch of hoarseness giving the man's tone a throaty sound.

Occupied in her task and still giggling to herself, Stacy tried to muster a growl. "You're ten minutes late."

"I—"

She cut him off unceremoniously. "Spare me the reasons. I have several other appointments today. Just get undressed."

"Get undressed?" His tone had risen at least an octave.

Frowning, Stacy tossed the damp toweling toward the wastepaper basket, missing it by a little less than a mile, and finally looked up at the man standing across the room.

Her frown immediately disappeared. "I do believe a miracle has just occurred." Walking closer, she scrutinized him intensely, carelessly setting her empty mug on the edge of the desk. Cupping her hand under her chin, she let her eyes travel slowly from his head to his slightly scuffed cordovan loafers. This was the man; the perfect image she'd fantasized about since taking on her latest assignment. The San Francisco Center for Humane Studies had commissioned her to sculpt a statue of fundamental man.

10

For more than two weeks she had been scouting for the right model. And here he was in the flesh. As she walked around him she muttered excitedly to herself, "Dark, but not too Mediterranean: a wonderful face, rugged and not pretty; good height, close to six feet probably; and even with your clothes on my guess is your body is perfect."

"Well, thanks." The stranger bestowed her an unabashed grin. "It's not often I meet a woman and get such an immediately complimentary and enthusiastic response."

"You have a good smile, too. The laugh lines form in all the right places. This just may be my lucky day."

"It may be mine as well." He laughed openly. His appreciative hazel eyes took in his admirer's delicate, animated features, her pert nose, sparkling honey brown eyes and the spun gold wisps of hair that kept escaping a haphazardly tied bandanna; only her mouth with those full, sensual lips disrupted the kittenish imagery. It gave Stacy English an enticingly provocative appeal, oversize smock and all.

Stacy, busy with her own observations, was oblivious to the stranger's inspection.

Caught off guard as she spun him in an about-face, he was astonished at the power in her grip. He continued the revolution, coming full circle to face her again.

"Let's not waste time," she said impatiently. "You

can throw your clothes over in the corner . . . uh
. . . what's your name?"

"Mike—"

"Mike." She nodded, not bothering to hear the last
name. What did it matter? This was the man she was
going to use as her model. It had been settled the
minute she set eyes on him. She reached behind her,
grabbing a sketch pad. Turning back to him, she saw
with consternation that he had not started to get
undressed.

As she glowered at him, Mike sighed resolutely
and slowly undid the buttons of his blue shirt.

Stacy watched restlessly as he moved at a snail's
pace. Then the light dawned.

"Don't tell me you never modeled in the nude
before?" She squinted her eyes in puzzled disbelief.
He didn't look like a novice.

Mike stopped at the next-to-last button. He
grinned again. Stacy noted that he had a very sexy
grin. Then, shaking her head to rid herself of the
thought, she brought herself to the business at hand.

"Actually . . . no," he murmured, his smile now
almost boyish.

"Well, don't feel shy," she said, her tone sympa-
thetic if somewhat surprised. She had found herself
a real natural, but she realized that she was going to
have to put her perfect find at ease. She smiled warmly. "The first time is always the hardest." As the
man's smile broadened, Stacy quickly added emphatically, "Modeling, I mean. Believe me, as far as

I'm concerned, you are nothing but lines, form and angles. Very good ones," she concluded, getting a glimpse through his open shirt of a well-muscled chest. Mike was a strikingly attractive man. Not only did his face have a rugged appeal; his beautifully masculine physique radiated potent sexuality. Those wavy locks of thick black hair, unruly and in need of a trim, also added to his earthy attraction. She saw a lot more than form as she looked at him, Stacy realized with a start. She'd need her head examined if she didn't. However, business was business.

Stacy cleared her throat in an attempt to clear her mind of her decidedly unprofessional analysis. She made it a rule not to fool around with models. These men invariably proved to be tediously vain and demanding, and Stacy rarely had anything in common with them.

She assisted Mike with the last button. Eager to get going, Stacy tugged the shirt off his shoulders.

"Think of me as your physician. Better still," she said with alacrity, "ignore me altogether."

"That's a tall order." He gazed at her admiringly. When Stacy groaned, preparing herself for his come-on, Mike said teasingly, "It's that white patch of clay on the tip of your nose. Very distracting."

He was original, she had to give him credit for that. Intentionally she kept her hands folded across her chest, determined not to find out if there really was a smudge on her nose. This was turning into a delicate situation, and Stacy was not good at diplomacy. But this guy was too perfect to lose. If she expressed too much irritation, he might just get huffy and decline the assignment. Models, Stacy had learned from enough experience, were annoyingly temperamental—the men worse than the women. It was not an easy task to bestow the right dosage of compliments and ego boosts while at the same time demanding a hands-off-the-artist policy. She would have to be especially careful with this already-reluctant poser. From that glint in his eye, she was well aware he had something other than modeling on his mind.

"Look . . . um, Mike. You really are exactly what I'm looking for. In fact, I am very amenable to paying you far more than the going rate if you take this assignment." She smiled with a touch of pleading in her warm, gold-flecked eyes. "I know you're feeling a little shy, but honestly, if you can simply think of me as a—a doctor . . ." she repeated.

"Okay." Mike capitulated, much to Stacy's relief. "As long as you'll think of me as your routine journalist."

"No problem," she muttered, paying scarce attention now that he had agreed to cooperate. Then the words penetrated. "What?" She did such a perfect double take that Mike chuckled loudly.

"Allow me to introduce myself formally," he said with a slight bow at the waist. "Mike Gallotti—onetime journalist; would-be model." The name rang a faint bell. Still she couldn't place it until Mike offered further information.

"Joe Turner, managing editor of the *New York Globe,* was supposed to get in touch with you. I'm doing the profile story on you and covering the unveiling of your *Peace and Harmony* sculpture at Government Plaza in two weeks. That is—unless your offer is better. You haven't told me how much you would pay—for my services."

"Very funny, Mr. . . ."

"Mike. Women rarely call me by my last name when I'm standing around half-undressed in their company."

Frowning as the bell in her head finally rang loudly, she muttered, "Joe did leave me some kind of garbled message on my answering machine." Joe Turner was a friend of her family, and Stacy had known him since she was a child. When she first started sculpting professionally, he had been one of her leading advocates. He always made sure that his paper gave all her new works a big spread in the art section. The last time she had spoken to him, he had suggested a profile piece for the Sunday magazine section to coincide with her latest work, but she had complained that she was too busy right now for a lengthy series of interviews. Obviously Joe had paid no attention to her refusal. Then again, he rarely paid attention if he'd already made up his mind. She should have known better, and she should have returned that phone message. Stacy sighed and looked up into Mike's teasing smile.

"Put your shirt on," she snapped, flinging her sketch pad angrily onto the worktable. The grimace turned to open disappointment in the next instant as she watched Mike reach for his shirt. He really did have a magnificent body.

"What if the price was right?" she asked with a spark of hope. Journalists didn't make all that much money.

"Sounds like a TV show my mother loves," he said with a laugh, slipping his arms into the sleeves. "I'm immensely flattered by all the compliments you've showered on me this morning, but the only time I care to be naked with a lovely young woman is when she follows suit. Unless, of course, that could be arranged."

"You don't look like an art critic," she said curtly. "And you don't come on like one, either. They're usually less obvious in their approach."

"You are very astute, English," he acknowledged with a mischievous grin, those shrewd hazel eyes sparkling. "The fact is, I'm not an art critic."

"Then what the hell are you?" she countered, her temper escalating rapidly. "And don't call me English. I don't like playing games, Mr. Gallotti." She put a sharp emphasis on the "Mr."

"I'm afraid," he nonchalantly continued, ignoring her slow boil, "art was not even one of my minors in the school I attended."

"And what school was that?" She raised a perfectly shaped eyebrow.

"School of the Streets. Also known as Hard-Knocks Academy. I doubt you ever heard of it."

Stacy found his supercilious tone even more irritating than his teasingly seductive style. "Why is that? Do you think hard knocks were only reserved for you?" she demanded.

"Let's see if I did my homework accurately: Williams Hall, a private day school until eighth grade; then Chilting Academy, an elegant boarding school in the Green Mountains of Vermont; a prestigious degree in art from Radcliffe College and, to round off your education, a year in Paris studying under one of France's top sculptors. Somehow I doubt the knocks were very hard in any of those spots."

"You know something, Mr. Gallotti," she said tartly, "it's really a pity. You would have been a perfect model for my next piece. But the only thing I hate more than a womanizer is someone who thinks he is holier than thou and lets you know it in insufferable detail."

"Didn't they teach you any manners in all those exclusive hallowed halls of education?"

"They taught me plenty. And just to round out your investigation of my background, you might like to learn that I've paid my dues, too." Stacy still vividly remembered some of the early reviews of her works that were frequently laced with patronizing remarks and clever quips about why someone so small needed to produce such massive sculptures. They may not have taken her seriously a few years ago, but she'd gotten the last laugh. Now she couldn't keep up with the requests for her work. But those early pans still got to her on occasion. She never had fully worked through accepting the kind of harsh criticism reviewers could dish out. She could see from the look in Mike's eyes that he was waiting for her to give him some specifics. No doubt; so he could give her another one of his patronizing smiles. Oh no, she thought, scowling, she was not about to give this infuriating man that satisfaction. Instead, she took the offensive.

"If you are not an arts reporter, why did Joe Turner send you here?" Before he could answer, she said firmly, "It doesn't matter. It's simply not going to work. Now if you'll leave, I have a lot of work to do and several more models to check out." And, she said to herself, I need to return my dear friend Joe's call and give him a piece of my mind—a large piece, she resolved. How could he have sent someone like Mike Gallotti to do this story?

"Believe me, English," he said dryly, intentionally accenting the last word, "I did not request this assignment. If Joe Turner weren't like a father to me and he could have gotten hold of any other living journalist to do this story, I would happily leave you to your obviously sexless preoccupation with the male body. Unfortunately, I'm in between assignments and I was the boss's only available candidate for this plum. A promise is a promise, and I always see a story through. Joe wants me to do a profile on you as well as a piece on the dedication of your sculpture, and he's going to get it. Now, do we cooperate or do we draw swords and duel to the death for the next two weeks?"

"Two weeks?" she echoed, forgetting his other remarks. "Impossible. My schedule is jam-packed."

"So I've read—in the society columns. You do get around, English. The opera, charity balls, theater opening nights, fashion shows . . . all attended on the arm of one dashing, sophisticated fellow after another. I don't think you've missed even one of the ten most eligible bachelors in the city during the last three months. You must be going for a record."

"I wouldn't have expected the society pages to interest you so much that you'd be able to keep such a precise accounting of my social activities."

"I believe in researching every possible detail before approaching a story."

"Well, despite what you might have unearthed in your studies, I do have other things to do besides keeping up with my busy social calendar. Foremost is the nude I've been commissioned to do. It's going to be one of my most complex pieces, and they want it by Christmas. That gives me exactly six months, and I haven't even found my model yet. That is, I found him, but he's not very obliging." The disappointed expression in her soulful brown eyes was obviously genuine. She still thought she had lost the ideal model for her sculpture.

"I'll make a deal with you," she said, her voice softer and more conniving. "You agree to pose, and I'll give you every detail of my life including step-by-step coverage of my scintillating encounters with every one of those eligible bachelors. It would make for some juicy reading," she quipped, "and I promise you won't have uncovered any of my rather interesting and frequently amusing tidbits in any of your research."

"It's a very appealing proposition. But it won't work unless you can do the piece of sculpture over the next two weeks. Your model is going to London on assignment then. How about this? You go about your business and I'll quietly tag along. Think of me—as invisible." His eyes, moments ago a soft hazel, now sparkled a vivid green.

"That would be about as easy as you imagining I'm your doctor." His provocative grin made her clarify her words. "I was referring to your mouth, Mr. Gallotti, not your body." No, this approach would get her nowhere. Despite his increasingly insufferable cockiness, Stacy was still determined to strike some kind of deal. She decided to switch tactics and try a new approach. "Let's start over, Mr. Gallotti."

"Mike," he reminded her, grinning. He had to hand it to her, she was tenacious. He was enjoying himself thoroughly.

"Mike," she agreed, forcing a sweet smile. "It's really very simple. I want something from you and you want something from me." She forced herself to ignore his provocative laugh. "Granted you only have two weeks. But you could pose for my preliminary sketches, and I'd get another model to fill in for the sculpture. In the meantime, you could get all the information you need for the profile. I promise to be very cooperative." Her voice trailed off as she smiled innocently at him.

"You ought to think about going into sales if you ever get tired of wielding a chisel. You have a terrific pitch." He tilted his chin at a slight angle. He had a way of looking sensually arrogant without even trying. Stacy began to worry about what she was getting herself into. Mike's infuriating smile as well as his careful scrutiny of her as he considered her offer was unnerving.

"Just what kind of journalist are you, anyway?" she asked, as much out of discomfort as curiosity.

"I see you read the front page of the *Globe* about as frequently as I scan the society pages. For your information, my byline does appear there on occasion." He threw her another one of his wry smiles. Stacy kept her irritation under wraps. Mike continued. "I don't suppose you have much interest in reading about all the misery in the world. You're much too busy." He caught the slight scowl across her forehead, but she quickly erased it. If he was hoping his deprecating tone would rile her, he didn't know whom he was dueling with.

"You're right. My work does keep me busy. Sculpting as well as my whirlwind social life just seem to take up too much of my time to sit around reading the paper. Why, it's been ages since I even had the chance to see how L'il Abner is doing in the comics section," she added with a thin smile.

"Society girl turned successful artist. I'm duly impressed." He cast her a sidelong glance and an indulgent nod.

"You should be," she said complacently, ignoring the teasing glint in his expressive eyes.

She was beginning to feel as if she was gaining some control over this farce. However, when he continued to stare, his look reflecting blatant amusement as well as interest, Stacy began to feel increasingly uncomfortable. His silence wasn't helping, and she could not muster up another thought—at least not one she cared to share with this infuriating yet devastatingly appealing man. If she had been able to stop thinking of him as the ideal prototype for her statue, she might have been better equipped to tune out her fantasies about what Mike Gallotti looked like without any clothes on. She had no doubt that if she gave him the slightest hint of desire, he would willingly oblige. If, of course, she was willing to reciprocate.

Stacy did not for one moment question her gut instincts. Mike Gallotti was not a man she felt safe getting involved with. Danger flashed all around him like glowing neon lights. She had an intuitive sense that were she to get involved, Mike Gallotti would not be someone she could easily forget. She started to feel relieved that he had not agreed to her offer. As good a model as he would be, she was beginning to see that if he took her up on her proposition, it could create too many difficulties.

Her relief was short-lived. Mike, standing so close that Stacy could feel his breath, said in a husky tone, "We haven't finalized our deal, English. The more I think about it, the more appealing it sounds."

Backing away to gain some emotional as well as physical distance, Stacy collided with a stool. A coffee cup, half hidden under a discarded smock, fell, splashing its contents onto the floor. "So that's where I put it." She laughed, glad of the distraction. As she bent to pick up the pieces, Mike's hand snaked out, catching her by the elbow.

"What do you say, English? Shall we shake on it?"

She was having trouble concentrating on what he was saying. His touch seemed to produce a tingling sensation that was somehow very disturbing. Straightening, she tried to restore her composure as she tugged her arm away.

"I don't know, Gallotti." She pursed her lips in a rueful expression. "You said yourself you don't know much about art. And besides, you—talk too much. You probably wouldn't keep your mouth shut long enough for me to do the sketches." She silently cursed the breathiness in her tone.

"Am I really that distracting?"

She knew she was fighting a losing battle. She also knew she was going to have to be careful. Mike Gallotti did a lot more than stir the artist in her. Where men were concerned, she was usually very cautious. A casual, unencumbered involvement was one thing. Losing one's heart was quite another. Staring into Mike's seductive gaze, she knew she would have to be constantly on her guard with him. Her better judgment told her to send him on his way, but her impulsive nature took over. Throwing caution to the winds, she said resolutely, "You've got yourself a deal. Besides, I owe it to Joe. He's always been in my corner."

"Terrific, English."

"The name's Stacy," she snapped, regretting her retort immediately. He obviously enjoyed trying to get her goat. Well, she mused, I'm just going to have to take Mike Gallotti down a peg or two. Let's see how quick his wit works when he's posing for me in his birthday suit. The image made her laugh out loud. She got the added pleasure of seeing her chuckle clearly throw Mike off guard for a moment. But he was quick to regain the offensive.

"Shall we start now?" he asked as he began to unbutton his shirt again.

Stacy needed some time to plan her own offense. "We can get going on the sketches tomorrow. But if you're really eager to start on the profile, you can meet me at Lincoln Center tonight at eight. A group of us are attending John Sevilla's opening-night concert, and we're going back to his hotel for drinks afterward. It will be a marvelous opportunity for you to get a glimpse of how the in-crowd really lives instead of having to read about it in tomorrow's society column," she said blithely.

"Something tells me, English, I'm going to learn a great deal from this assignment." He looked at her seductively, then grinned. "Lincoln Center at eight."

As he started to leave, Stacy said pointedly, "Oh, and it's formal. Do you have . . ."

"Never fear. I will dig through my closet until I come up with something other than khaki pants. I promise not to embarrass you or your important friends. See you at eight with rings on my fingers, bells on my toes and a black tie neatly bowed around my neck." He blew her a kiss and sauntered out the door.

Stacy decided to give Joe Turner a piece of her mind after all. She may have struck a fair enough deal with the smug Mr. Gallotti, but she had a feeling the balance could easily tip in his favor if she didn't watch out. She wanted every detail she could collect on Mike Gallotti so that she would be well armed. As she reached under a mass of papers for her phone book, she discovered the other missing coffee cup, which had been balanced on the edge of the book. Ruefully Stacy wiped the wet cover off on her jeans and then looked up Joe's phone number.

CHAPTER TWO

"Slow down, Stacy. What's all the fuss about, anyway?" Joe's voice crackled over the phone. He tried to sound soothing, but he was obviously not happy at this interruption. Still, he was fond of Stacy, her fiery temper notwithstanding. "I told you, sweetheart." Stacy could hear him exhaling cigar smoke as he talked. "Bennett is out sick, and damn near every other reporter on this paper is tied up. Everyone of quality, that is. Now you wouldn't want some cub doing your profile?"

"But Joe . . ." Stacy could see she wasn't going to get anywhere. Still, she persisted. "Really—a news journalist? What the hell does he know about art, anyway? I'll tell you—nothing."

"Don't you worry, honey. He's going to do a first-class job. He always does. He's been with me since he was wet behind the ears straight out of high school. That's almost twenty years. Believe me, this is going to be a piece of cake. No problem." He really wasn't convinced of that. Knowing both Stacy and Mike as well as he did, he had a feeling there were going to be plenty of problems. Chuckling softly, he kept his thoughts to himself.

"I give up," Stacy said with a groan. "But the next time you decide to do a story on me, you'd better make sure first that Bennett or whatever other art critic you've got is healthy and on the job."

"Scout's honor," he promised, relieved to get this problem settled. As he started to say good-bye, Stacy put in the last word.

"And I warn you, Joe, I want to see whatever this Gallotti writes about me before it goes to press."

"Absolutely. But don't you worry. Mike is going to be great."

Just why was Joe Turner laughing when he hung up the phone, Stacy wondered. She failed to see anything amusing about these next two weeks with Mike Gallotti.

She put down the phone but lifted it again almost at once, and dialed.

"Sam, it's Stacy. Do you still have your stack of old *Globes* lying around?"

"You know I don't believe in throwing useless things out," he said and laughed into the receiver.

"Good. I'll be over in a few minutes."

She threw off her smock and slipped on a short-sleeved red-and-white-striped jersey. As she flew down the stairs, she remembered she was still wearing her bandanna. Stuffing it into her back pocket, she ran her fingers through her short, curly blond hair. Stacy hated primping. Every few months she dropped into the local hairdresser and told him to cut. Her hair was so thick and healthy that even the plainest of styles looked elegant on her. It always astonished Stacy that her ultrachic friends, who spent hours at the most renowned beauty salons in the city, were convinced that she had a secret hairdresser locked away for her own personal use.

Stacy was something of an oddity among her crowd. Her standard outfit of jeans and jersey tops certainly seemed almost dowdy compared to the designer clothes her friends always wore. She could, of course, dress beautifully when duty called. But her wardrobe consisted of only a few basic outfits. She found shopping a waste of time, and being slender and petite, she looked good in almost anything. Stacy took advantage of this as well as her artistic talent to fashion unique outfits out of common, inexpensive materials. Again, friends demanded to know her secret dress designer.

Stacy had been reared to play the sophisticated upper-class young woman. She knew the role by heart and acted it when necessary. But inside, she was naturally avant-garde and bohemian. None of her odd ways ultimately mattered, she knew. She had learned long ago that when you came from old money and were well schooled, being a bit eccentric was considered almost charming.

Stacy viewed the world she came from as "designer plastic." The artificiality used to get to her, but for the most part she had come to disassociate herself mentally from the scene. It made participating in the activities that still interested her a great deal easier. Her real world began and ended in her studio, where she opened her soul and unearthed masterful sculptures hidden beneath stone and marble slabs.

Sam Collins's studio was less than a block from Stacy's. He and Stacy had met five years ago, when they had shared an art showing in Greenwich Village. Sam also worked on a massive scale, but his art was created with oils on canvas. The two had hit it off from the start and had been good friends ever since. Sam played the part of the eccentric artist to the hilt. His manner was outrageous and he dressed with a calculated flamboyance. Buying much of his wardrobe at secondhand stores, Sam frequently strolled about the streets in the most incredibly mismatched outfits Stacy had ever seen. With his carrot-red hair hanging well past his shoulders and an exotic handlebar mustache, he was quite a sight.

Stacy adored him. He was the only artist she knew who was not beset by the frequent mood swings that creative people are prone to. Sam Collins must have been born under a rising sun, Stacy thought. He was the most consistently cheerful person she had ever run into. A few of her sophisticated friends who had met Sam laughingly claimed his marvelous good spirits had to be due to some emotional or mental defect. But Stacy knew otherwise and valued his friendship above that of almost anyone she knew.

"Hi, Mutt," he greeted her with a flashing smile. Over six feet tall, Sam was always amused by the contrast in their height and had nicknamed her Mutt early in their relationship.

"Nice," Stacy said enthusiastically as she walked over to Sam's newest creation. "Fabulous motion—and color. I love it."

"Me too," he agreed. "It's my symbolic representation of the first time Annie took me to that disco on West Eighty-sixth Street. Everyone was a whirl of movement, whizzing about in Technicolor garishness. I do believe I've captured the event to a T," Sam said and grinned.

"Now that you explain, I really can see dancers whizzing about." Stacy chuckled. "Yes indeed, this painting is bound for glory."

"I'll settle for the Museum of Modern Art," he returned dryly.

"Where's Annie?" Stacy asked, not seeing Sam's girlfriend about.

"Oh, she's down at Emilio's or some other coffee house, drowning her sorrows in an iced chocolate," he said lightly.

"What's her problem?" Stacy asked absently, not particularly concerned about the frequently sullen

Annie. She always found it amazing that Sam and Annie were a pair. Their personalities were so different. Annie was as tense and moody as Sam was cheerful and optimistic. Oh well, she thought, there's never any accounting for taste.

Sam leisurely blended a few oils and said in his typical offhand style, "She's mad because I won't take her to see *Night of the Stalking Dead.* She claims it's a true masterpiece, but she's too scared to go alone. I told her after holding her hand through *Creatures of Planet X* and having nightmares for the next two nights that she was not going to get me into any more of those ridiculous horror flicks. She'll pout for a while, come back with resolute acceptance, ask me to forgive her, and then—we'll go catch the late showing." He threw Stacy a sly grin.

"Why make her go through all that torment if you're going to give in to her in the end?" she scolded him lightly.

"Ah, Mutt, there are so many things in the world of love that you don't understand. One of these days you are going to have to take the plunge and discover what true *amore* is all about." He teasingly ruffled her hair.

"I will never figure out, Sam Collins, how you can handle love and creativity at the same time. I know I can't."

"That, my darling Mutt, is because you take both art and love too seriously. I am convinced seriousness is the artist's worst sin. Come to think of it, I think that's true for everyone." He grinned, pleased with his homespun philosophy.

"Well, I sure wish some of your joviality would rub off on me. Especially today."

"Why? You having some trouble?" he asked.

"I'm not sure yet," she said. "Where are those stacks of newspapers you so carefully preserve?"

"Last I saw of them there were a couple of stacks under the counter in the kitchen. Annie keeps threatening to throw them out."

Stacy was in luck. She found the last several weeks' worth of *Globe*s neatly piled in the kitchen.

As she began sifting through them, carefully ripping out selected articles from each, Sam strolled over.

"Since when did you get such an avid interest in world events?" he teased. "Aren't you the girl who once told me, 'What's the point of reading depressing news when there's usually enough going on in your own life to feel miserable about'?"

"You have a photographic memory, my friend, to add to all your other attributes." She smiled. "I still feel the same way."

"So what's this little collection of newsworthy items all about?"

"I'm just doing a bit of research," she muttered, checking the last paper in the stack. Tearing off the article in the upper right hand column and its continuation on page 8, she gathered her clippings, folded them neatly and put them in her front pocket.

"Tell me, Sam, do you read all these papers or simply collect them for posterity?"

"Unlike yourself, reading about everyone else's suffering always makes me feel that much more content with my own meager life." He tweaked her nose affectionately.

"Have you ever heard of a journalist by the name of Mike Gallotti?" She tried to sound casual, but Sam gave her a curious look.

"Mike Gallotti, huh?" His dark brown eyes narrowed. "So that's whose news articles you've been furiously tearing out. Don't tell me you've just become another member of Gallotti's fan club," he said with surprise.

"You mean he's that popular?"

"Where there is danger and action, there is Mike Gallotti. Annie, for one, adores him. He's on public TV a lot—on those news shows where they have reporters from different papers around the country discussing world events. Annie claims he's the sexiest-looking reporter she's ever seen. I gather many women share her point of view and would love getting their clutches on the man. Rumor has it that more than a few already have."

"You seem to know a lot about him."

"You don't read newspapers, and you don't watch TV. No wonder the Great Gallotti is unknown to you," he said with mock dismay. "Besides, as I said, I live with one of his most ardent fans. You know Annie—once she gets onto something, I hear about it constantly. Also, the man happens to be one of the most respected and admired hard-news journalists in this country. He's got some kind of mad, fearless streak in him that allows him to risk life and limb for a story. How he has held onto either all these years is one of the true miracles of the age."

Stacy felt an involuntary shiver streak down her spine. Sam's description of Mike was completely at odds with the rather lightweight view of him she had gotten, despite Joe Turner's exalted praise of Gallotti.

Back at her studio a little while later, as she read through all the clippings, Stacy understood even more what Sam had been telling her. Mike really had taken awesome risks to cover some of the stories he wrote for the *Globe*. He might not be much of an art critic, but he was one hell of a newspaperman. Stacy found herself wishing he weren't.

She was standing on the plaza in front of Avery Fisher Hall at Lincoln Center by a few minutes after eight. Almost compulsively punctual, Stacy was always annoyed by her friends' habit of arriving fashionably late for everything. It was, she thought, yet another thing that set her apart from them. Stacy had to admit, though, that part of the reason she could always be on time was that she simply refused to spend hours dressing and applying makeup. It usually took her less than a half hour from shower to front door. Another reason Stacy was never late

34

was that she was naturally considerate. It was just part of her personality. When she made plans to be somewhere, she was there on time—invariably waiting for others to show up.

It wasn't that she minded hanging around waiting for her companions. She was always happy to have an opportunity to watch other people, and tonight was no exception. With over five events going on in the various opulent buildings in the center, there was enough action to keep Stacy happily interested forever. Every type of human being she could imagine could be found among the milling crowd on this balmy summer night. Stacy loved New York City. Its energy and vitality never failed to delight her.

She didn't recognize him at first, and from the surprised look in his eye as he casually walked over to her, she guessed he hadn't recognized her right away either. Elegantly dressed in a well-tailored black evening suit, crisp white shirt and bow tie, as promised, Mike Gallotti practically took her breath away.

"As I live and breathe—it's Cinderella in the flesh." He flashed her a pearly white smile. "And what flesh," he added, lightly touching her bare arm and shoulder. She was wearing a beautiful ivory satin evening dress that was softly draped in front and low slung in back. Fitted at her narrow waist with a delicately woven gold belt, the skirt fell gently around her hips, ending just below her knees. Thin-strapped high-heeled sandals brought Stacy up to his shoulders. She had to be the most exquisite woman he had ever set his eyes on, Mike thought as he stared at her. He could not remember wanting any woman more.

Stacy was also feeling strongly attracted to Mike, but her uncertainty and wariness about him prevented her from enjoying the sensual images flitting through her mind. Instead, she pretended to scan the crowd intensely.

"My friends are usually late, I'm afraid," she explained, keeping her eyes on the people gathered about the plaza. "They make it a point to miss at least the first part of any performance. It's a shame tonight. Sevilla is premiering his newest work. It really is important to hear it from the beginning to get the full force of the whole piece . . ."

"You're rambling, English." He cocked his head to one side, studying her through narrowed eyes. "Why are you so nervous? Don't I look presentable enough for the jet set?"

She smiled wryly as she brought her gaze back to him. "I thought only women fished for compliments. You look terrific—suave, sophisticated, urbane. You will put my jet-set friends to shame. There, did I boost your ego enough, Mr. Gallotti?"

"You boosted it more this morning. I suppose I have to be at least half naked to bring back that vibrant excitement in those big brown eyes of yours."

"Mike, let's make a deal. I won't give you a hard time if you will stop giving me one. My only interest in you this morning was that you were the perfect prototype for my sculpture—nothing more."

"And now? What's your interest now?"

"Every successful artist needs good press. The profile and coverage on my *Peace and Harmony* sculpture will be good for business. Plus I get you to model for me," she added, smiling. "More to the point, Gallotti, what is your interest?" she asked coolly.

He scrutinized her with the same intensity with which she had examined him that morning. "You know something, English—I'm not really sure." His craggy face took on a bemused look. "You could be the most dangerous assignment I've ever taken on."

For a brief moment their facades lifted and they looked straight into each other's eyes. What Mike said was true for them both. The walls they had each so painstakingly erected to protect themselves over the years had begun to crack the minute they set eyes on each other. Stacy wondered with a sense of panic just what it would take to plaster hers up again.

"Sevilla is a phenomenal composer. Are you familiar with any of his works?" Her mask was back in place. He grinned at the switch, but right now he was as relieved as Stacy to shift gears.

Mike was as committed as Stacy to keeping himself unencumbered, and he knew that was the secret of his success as a journalist. He was always willing to take any risk necessary to get a story, because he had no one to consider but himself. He had seen enough reporters in his day who got married and had kids, ending up having to weigh each assignment carefully because of their other responsibilities. Mike didn't hold it against them. Occasionally he even envied them. But he had spent twenty years working his way up to his present position, and he was not going to jeopardize it.

"Racing around the world, unfortunately, gives me little time to keep up with new composers. Lucky I took this story. I might never have gotten the opportunity to attend one of his concerts otherwise."

She knew he was being facetious, but she refused to rise to the bait. "I think a little culture might actually do you a world of good. Shall we go in? I don't want to miss the opening movement."

"Absolutely." He grinned. "Neither would I."

They had front-row-center orchestra seats. After the first two minutes of the opening movement, Stacy heard Mike groan quietly. She shot him a quick glance and grinned. He smiled back at her, trying to act attentive. The music was so drearily atonal and shrill that Mike couldn't have fallen asleep if he had wanted to. He concentrated instead on not yawning or fidgeting. He could be as sophisticated as the next guy—or die trying.

By the second movement, which Mike decided, much to his amazement, was even worse than the first, he was fast running out of steam. He had given up smoking five years ago, but right now all he could think about was having a dozen cigarettes in the lobby while Sevilla screeched out the last two movements. Stacy's companions showed up just as he was about to excuse himself, feigning a trip to the men's room. Sighing as her friends wedged him in, he sat it out, praying for intermission. His stiffly starched collar was irritating his neck, and the heavily perfumed woman next to him was irritating his senses.

Intermission was more draining than Sevilla's noise. He stood near the sophisticated group as they raved about the performance. Stacy was relatively quiet, although she made a few remarks that indicated her appreciation.

Mike had never felt more out of his element. He was not ignorant when it came to music. In his self-education, he had come to appreciate good jazz and the fine classical composers. But this music tonight was completely foreign to him. Either everyone in the theater who had applauded so wildly was crazy, or he was.

By the end of the concert, Mike was convinced it was everyone else who was insane—or else they were hell-bent on going along with something simply because it was considered "in." These ultrachic jet-setters had to be a part of what was "in" regardless of what the thing was.

After the concert one of Stacy's friends had a chauffeured limo waiting to take them to the Plaza for a cocktail party in honor of Sevilla. Stacy knew that Mike would have loved to beg off, but she purposely gave him no opportunity to do so. He had told her he wanted to be her shadow, and she was going to see to it that he stuck it out to the bitter end. Not at all sadistic by nature, she had to admit she was getting a certain satisfaction from his quiet suffering.

The party was already under way when they arrived, even though Sevilla had not yet made his grand entrance. When the composer finally showed up twenty minutes later, he was greeted by a chorus of applause and bravos. He swept into the room, bowing, shaking hands and kissing the women. Mike noticed with amusement that he kissed the pretty ones full on the lips, and the dowdy ones got a peck on the cheek. Each of them seemed thrilled with whatever the grand master bequeathed to them. Standing off on the sidelines, Mike desperately looked around for the cute little waitress who was carrying a tray of champagne glasses. He decided he was going to need several to get through this event.

He didn't manage to get the drink. Stacy came over to him and grabbed his hand, dragging him to the small group that were listening in rapt attention to the maestro discussing the deep inner meaning behind his newest creation.

Mike listened quietly for a couple of minutes. Sevilla was gesturing dramatically, his voice raised in excitement, when Mike, extracting his hand from Stacy's, reached out and grabbed Sevilla's in a firm handshake.

Sevilla stood there dumbfounded at the interruption as Mike vigorously shook his hand. "Good going, old man. Really. Very delightful. I can't wait for Part Two. Hate to dash like this but we simply must . . ."

Releasing Sevilla's limp hand, he again took hold of Stacy's, which was now clutched somewhere between her chest and throat in horrified disbelief. Before she could catch her breath, they were outside in the hall. She stood there frozen as Mike pressed the button for the elevator.

Finally getting her voice back, she said frostily, "That had to be the rudest, most insufferable behavior I have ever witnessed."

"I couldn't agree more." He smirked. "The only thing more insufferable than Sevilla's music is the man himself," he added, watching her fume at his intentional misunderstanding of her accusation.

Stacy's look of annoyance lasted for exactly ten seconds. Then giggles started to erupt despite her struggles to stifle them. She soon gave up trying to fight it, her laughter bursting out and echoing loudly through the high-ceilinged hallway. Mike's own hearty chuckles joined hers. Clutching him as tears of laughter sprang from her eyes, Stacy tried to catch her breath. "Did you see the expression on his face when you started pumping his hand?" she managed to get out before she once again dissolved in laughter. They roared hysterically all the way down in the elevator to the main floor of the hotel. The people getting in as they stepped out into the lobby regarded them with dignified disdain.

The fresh air calmed them both. Stacy wiped away her tears and Mike took a deep breath.

"You are crazy." She grinned at him.

"You're beautiful," he responded softly, all the laughter gone from his face. He moved toward her, his hands gently clasping her shoulders, and brushed his lips gently against hers. Stacy smiled hesitantly at him as he stepped back. Then, throwing caution to the winds, she moved toward him, threw her arms around his neck and brought his lips down for a second round.

Mike's long fingers pressed against her bare back as he drew her up to him for a kiss that was far more passionate and hungry than the first. Stacy's lips parted to receive his exploring tongue. She clung to him, afraid that if he let go, her legs would never hold her. She was right. When he pulled back from the embrace, she almost lost her balance. He gripped her arms tightly, still keeping his distance.

"I haven't necked with a girl on the street since I was fifteen," he said with a smile. "Come on, let's go."

Stacy still felt giddy as Mike hailed a taxi. It had only been a brief embrace, a simple kiss. There was certainly no reason to start falling apart. Still, her pulse was racing wildly; she felt disturbingly quivery, and she hadn't even thought to ask him where they were going.

Their cab pulled up in front of Molly's Bar and Grill. Stacy threw him a questioning look as he helped her out of the taxi.

"I thought I'd show you how the other half lives—and eats. Personally, black fish eggs, chopped liver and champagne do not a meal make for this fellow. I don't know about you, but I'm starving."

Stacy quickly hid her surprise and a twinge of disappointment behind a wide smile. "What's Molly's specialty—humble pie?"

As they walked into the pub, she told herself that she was glad Mike hadn't taken advantage of her after she had dropped her guard. She had by now returned to her senses. Only her body, still aroused, betrayed her desire.

Molly's was bustling, and Stacy had to shout to be heard over the din.

"It will quiet down in a few minutes, once the third shift at the *Globe* goes on duty," he shouted back when she asked if it was always this frenetic.

Mike returned greetings to just about every man in the place. Their reaction to her ranged from discreetly interested glances to overtly lascivious stares. She quickly realized that she was the only woman in the place and found herself hoping that Molly would appear just so she wouldn't feel absolutely outnumbered. However, Mike cheerfully informed her that Molly died fifty years ago, and Ray Flannigan had been running this place for the better part of the last twenty years.

A varied assortment of Mike's cronies kept popping over to their table. Reporter's jargon, Stacy discovered, had much in common with a foreign language. A fair amount of it was certainly unintelligible to her. Still, once she let herself relax, she found that she liked quite a few of the reporters with their glib tongues and sharp wits. She was even beginning to get used to their lustful looks, feeling a little flattered. The mood in Molly's was cheerful and good-natured, and Stacy couldn't help but enjoy herself.

By the time Stacy took the last savory bite of the best beef stew she had ever tasted, she was having a wonderful time. The noise had died down a bit, as Mike had promised, but there was still plenty of life about. After the third shift departed, a few reporters crowded around their small table, each one trying to top the other in telling jokes, their sole aim being to hear Stacy laugh. She obliged every one of them and even told a few amusing stories herself.

"Your friends are very funny," she said when they were finally left alone over coffee.

"They liked you, too." He grinned. "Remind me the next time I take you here to make sure you are more than half-dressed first. Those poor guys are going to have a hell of a time fitting their eyes back into their heads tonight."

"Well, I also had little competition in this place," she said demurely.

"English, you wouldn't have competition if the

Miss America pageant walked through those doors," he said with a laugh.

"It's nice to see you can dish out compliments as well as take them."

Tipping his chair back against the wall, he folded his hands across his chest and contemplatively stared at her. His gaze held her fixed, her eyes watching his in turn.

Sighing deeply, he leaned forward, making the chair thump back onto all four legs, and he gently took her hand.

"How can one little lady be so many different women? You've really got me baffled. But I'll tell you something. Before the next two weeks are up, I plan to discover the real Stacy English."

Stacy met his lazily sensual gaze. "And am I going to unearth the real Mike Gallotti?"

CHAPTER THREE

During the taxi ride to Stacy's loft Mike lightly rested his arm around her shoulder, his fingers gently caressing her satiny smooth skin. All Stacy's instincts were telling her to be wary. She tried to make small talk to ease the tension that was building inside her.

Mike's teasing smile told her he knew what she was doing. And it was clear he had no intention of making things easy for her. His dark hazel eyes provocatively watched her struggle to come up with topics. Meanwhile his fingers continued their increasingly sensual strokes.

Stacy knew the score. He was winding up for the finale. That smug, self-assured look in his eyes left no doubt about what he wanted—and what he assumed he would get. Well, she thought with an inner smile, Mr. Gallotti is about to be taken down his first peg. Thinking about what his expression would be when she gave him a firm, no-nonsense good night in the cab helped more than anything else to offset the tantalizing feel of his touch.

It was all set in Stacy's mind. The cab pulled up in front of her building. She turned to him and started to say good night as planned when she noticed something different in his gaze. The cockiness was gone. In its place she saw a flicker of puzzlement and agitation. Stacy suddenly forgot her resolve. Instead, she found herself asking softly, "Would you like to come up for a drink or something?"

"Or something?" he teased, his eyes again amused and his grin victorious. But then the look vanished. In a husky, slightly hesitant voice he said, "I'll have a drink."

The old commercial elevator in the converted warehouse building ground to a halt, and the metal door slowly opened. Mike reached for the handle of the iron mesh inner door, sliding it out of the way and ushering Stacy inside. All the way up to the top floor they had kept their eyes focused on the small numbers that flashed sequentially as they made their ascent.

Stacy took the keys from her purse and, fumbling, unlocked the two bolts and the alarm system. The process seemed endless. Finally she swung the door open and stepped inside. Mike followed.

"What would you like—to drink?" she asked softly, flicking on the light switch as they walked inside.

"I think I'd better stick to coffee," he said.

Stacy busied herself in the kitchen making a fresh pot. She stood watching the bubbling brew slowly drip down into the carafe. Her hands were trembling as she reached for the cups. She felt a wave of regret for having asked Mike in. How could her life suddenly feel so complicated? Was it really only today that Mike had ambled through that door? No man had ever made such an impact on her. He could infuriate her faster than anyone she knew. And he could also cause her body to go haywire despite all her silent warnings.

How was she ever going to manage to keep this relationship casual? Not only was she wildly attracted to Mike, she had even begun worrying about him. Sam had said that Mike was the supreme daredevil of journalism. He constantly put himself in danger—often risked his life. She couldn't afford to start worrying about when his luck was finally going to run out. The thought made her ill.

She wished she could adopt her friend Sam's philosophy of not taking anything too seriously. But Stacy was—and always had been—an intense person. She was also a dedicated artist. She never allowed anything to get in the way of her concentration. Once she began a piece, she became lost in her work, her mind clear of all thoughts other than what lay beneath the surface of the stone. She would not abide any man disturbing that concentration.

No, she told herself with a newly found confidence, this thing with Mike was never going to work. She would walk in there, tell him exactly how she felt and suggest that his boss find someone else to do this story. It would be better to get him out of her life right now, before it was too late. The hell with their deal. She decided she probably wouldn't be able to keep her disturbing fantasies in control long enough to sketch him.

Her latest resolve never made it past the kitchen. As she walked into the studio and saw Mike carefully studying one of her sculptures, all determination vanished. He wasn't aware that she was watching him. With graceful gestures he ran his fingers lightly over the piece—a delicate dove in flight—feeling the cool smoothness and fluid curves. As she stood there silently observing him while he so sensuously traced the sculpted marble form, all she could think about was what it would be like to feel those fingers tracing her body, caressing her skin. She desperately wished at that moment that she could forget all her doubts and allow herself what she was certain would be an exquisite experience. If he was to turn now, walk over to her, and take her in his arms, she would be lost.

He did turn around at that very moment and walk to her. But his hands only reached out for one of the mugs of coffee. Stacy released her breath.

"You're a fine sculptor. That piece is wonderful. It has a majestic grace that's very moving. I'd love to own something that beautiful. Maybe I'll commission you one of these days to do a sculpture for me. It wouldn't have to be . . ."

"You're rambling, Gallotti. What's the matter? You nervous?" They both laughed.

"What are we doing here?" he asked so abruptly that Stacy swallowed her hot coffee too quickly and coughed.

"I'm not sure," she answered truthfully, setting her cup down and perching on a nearby stool. "I can't figure you out, Mike. What concerns me is how much I find myself wanting to."

"We seem to be on the same wavelength." Mike took her hand and led her to a couch. "When Joe threw this assignment at me, I had a fit. I've never done an art review in my life, and it's been more years than I can remember since I've done profiles and human interest stories. This assignment was a piece of fluff as far as I could see." Before she could balk, he went on. "It's not turning out that way." He shrugged his shoulders and looked straight into her eyes. "I'm a newsman. I've risked life and limb more often than I care to remember to get a story. Believe me, I've done some crazy things in my day." There was a small smile on his lips. "This may be the craziest." He pushed a stray lock of hair away from his eyes. "You asked back at Molly's whether you were going to figure out who I really am. Well, here are some straight-from-the-shoulder facts. I'm a hard-nosed news hound who likes being responsible to no one but myself. I go where I want, do what I want, and I don't answer to anyone. And given my life-style, I can't afford any serious involvements. I'll tell you, English, when the old heart starts to flutter, I beat a fast retreat. It's the one danger I've made a point of always avoiding."

Stacy smiled. He could have been taking the words right out of her mouth.

Mike cast her a wistful look. "So how come I'm sitting here with you, shaking like a leaf inside. My head is telling me I ought to run like hell. The problem is, I have never found a woman more irresistible." In a husky whisper he added, "And more threatening." His eyes, a brilliant green now, held hers. His look alone made her own heart produce some potent flutters.

A little breathless, Stacy murmured, "You scare the hell out of me, too."

She stood up and walked to the window. The distance did not lessen the electric current that connected them.

"The fact is, Gallotti," she said, trying to sound as cool and in control as possible and praying that the insistent pulsating sensation in her stomach would settle down, "I can't afford you, either. It's too big a price to pay." She sat down on the window seat. "I'm as independent and as dedicated to keeping myself that way as you. An artist simply can't afford complicated relationships. They take up too much energy, require too much work. Maybe a few artists manage it," she said, thinking of Sam and Annie, "but I can't. All my energy is wrapped up in my sculpting. I don't have any left over—and I can't spare what I've got to let myself get entangled in a relationship." She caught hold of the window-shade cord, unconsciously twirling it around her index finger. "All my life I knew I was going to be an artist. My parents humored me. It wasn't that they thought I had no talent. They believed I was good. But they never imagined a young woman raised with every imaginable advantage including a hefty trust fund would give up the beautiful life to hole up in a loft and hack away at stone eighteen hours a day. I've worked damn hard to get where I am, and I did it on my own. I suffered plenty of bruises along the way, especially to my ego. But I don't regret one moment of it. I'm doing exactly what I want to be doing. And until you walked through that door this morning, nothing has come close to complicating my plans." She looked across at him, a wry smile curving her lips.

Mike walked over. Standing in front of her, he skimmed his palm along her cheek. "Maybe we're starting to unravel our real selves already. It's turning out that we are a lot alike—dedicated, independent, hot-tempered, stubborn . . ."—he sat down next to her—"madly attracted to one another and scared as hell." He took hold of her chin and turned her face to his. Slowly he brought his lips toward hers and kissed her tenderly. His mouth felt warm, gentle, loving—and filled with promise.

When he drew back, Stacy sighed. "This is crazy. We both know we're heading for big trouble. Please, Mike . . . ?" She was not at all sure what she was asking. Her body was in an all-out war with her mind. As he leaned toward her to kiss her again, he whispered, "Trouble is my middle name."

He gathered her in his arms, all his own resolutions to keep away forgotten in his passion. He never could keep away from danger. Why should this be any different?

But even as those thoughts flew threw his mind, he knew this was different. Then all thought vanished as she slipped her arms around his neck, folding her body against him.

Her mouth eagerly met his, her fingers digging into the hard muscles of his back. He felt so strong, so vital. She was intoxicated by the feel of him, the musky scent of his aftershave adding to the almost drunken sensation she felt. Lost in a desire that was already out of control, she let a hungry moan escape her lips.

It was Mike who pulled back. She could see the pained expression in his face, feel his warm breath as he exhaled heavily.

"Oh Stacy, you feel too damn good. And you make me feel too good." He took hold of her shoulders. "I could get used to this feeling. Much too used to it."

Stacy didn't say a word. She couldn't. Her heart was still racing; her body still throbbed. She had pushed aside all her fears and resolves because she wanted him despite all reason. But Mike had held onto some of his. She was filled with an odd mixture of anger and relief when he released her.

"I'd better get out of here," he said huskily, letting go of her shoulders, "before there's no way out." He stood up but didn't move away. "I won't give you odds on my stopping next time around. We'd both better be on our best behavior from here on out." He jauntily tilted his head to the side, but his eyes still held her gaze.

"I can be as good as you," she replied, trying to calm herself.

Mike grinned. "I'll bet you can." He walked to the door. "Thanks for that cup of coffee, Stacy."

After he left, she took the two full mugs and emptied them into the sink.

Stacy was in the middle of a pleasant dream when the phone rang. Yawning, she sleepily picked up the receiver.

"Stacy, this is Joe . . . Joe Turner. What the hell is going on?"

"What are you talking about?" It took her a few seconds to clear her head enough to realize whom

54

she was talking to. She sat up in bed, wide awake now.

"Mike just called me and asked me—no, damnit, he begged me to take him off this assignment. What did you do to the guy, anyway?" he snarled. "First you get on my back to get him off the story. Now he's doing the same thing. What gives?"

Ignoring his question, her muscles tensing, she asked quietly, "What did you tell him?" She wasn't sure what she wanted to hear.

"What did I tell him? I told him that if he could risk fires, floods and wars, he certainly could risk coming up against one peanut of a girl, for God's sake."

"He—he's still on the story, then," she said hoarsely, her throat gone dry.

"Of course he's still on the story. Look, Stacy, I know each of you pretty well. You and Mike are both hot-tempered, sarcastic, stubborn devils. But I expect you both to behave yourselves. This spread Mike is going to do will put the name Stacy English on the top of the heap and don't you forget it. Just be nice and cooperate. If Gallotti steps out of bounds, you give me a buzz and I'll handle him."

"Don't worry, Joe," Stacy said emphatically. "There won't be any further—complications."

Hanging up the receiver, Stacy sank back on her pillows. She was no longer the least bit tired, but she was too caught up in a flood of emotions to get out of bed. She tried to sort out her feelings. On the top of the pile was anger. Why the hell had he given her that speech about behaving themselves for the next two weeks if his plan was to skip out? Of course, in all fairness, she had to admit that she had wanted him taken off the story too. Wouldn't it have been better if Joe had given in to them? There was no doubt it would have made things a lot easier. So why was she still fuming? Because, she admitted, the thought of never seeing Mike again made her feel awful. And, she added, throwing off the covers, she wasn't the one behaving like a coward. And she had as much to lose as Mike if they didn't behave themselves. She knew she was strong enough to see this assignment through. So, she thought, let's see how strong the fiercely independent, unencumbered Mike Gallotti is going to be now that he was stuck with her.

Once she had focused on the challenge, she felt a lot better. After all, she was already one up on Mike. He had placed that last call to Joe. He was the one trying to escape, not she. She managed to push aside the twinges of hurt that snuck up on her, the feeling of rejection when she realized Mike really would have run off had Joe agreed. She told herself it was merely a bruise to her pride. She knew she was lying, but it helped anyway.

After showering and slipping on her standard uniform of jeans and a jersey, this one a bold yellow tank top, Stacy downed a glass of orange juice and a slightly burned piece of toast. Walking over to her worktable, she started doing some freehand sketches. Her mind was clear enough about what she wanted, but her hands wouldn't cooperate. After several poor attempts she tore up the drawings in frustration. She closed her eyes, letting herself fantasize devilish little schemes to make Mike squirm. When Joe had told her to behave herself, he had had no idea just how well behaved she planned to be. Poor Mike, she thought as she smiled slyly to herself. He, too, was in for a big surprise. If he thought he wanted out now, just wait until she really started going to work.

Her fantasies were disturbed by a knock on her door. She walked across the room and opened it. Mike greeted her with a warm, cheerful good morning and walked into the room. Crossing to her desk, he glanced at the pile of torn papers. "No success this morning?" he quipped.

Stacy did not waste any time on pleasantries. In her coolest, most efficient voice, she said, "I like to start sketching by eight. So try to get here by that time from now on. Now if it isn't asking too much, would you mind getting undressed so that we can start?"

"My, my, English. You really are hell-bent on getting my clothes off."

"I'm not in the mood for your glib wit this morning. And having you continue to refer to me as English does not help my humor any. Don't tell me you're getting cold feet. We do still have a deal, don't we?"

She was giving him his chance to come clean. She would feel far less hostile if he would admit he wanted to get out of this assignment and had called Joe.

Mike only sighed. "I never welch on a deal."

Okay, Gallotti, if that's the way you want to play it, Stacy said silently. To him, she said, "Good. I hate welchers. Let's get to work."

"Uhh, when do I get all those scintillating details you promised?"

"Don't worry, I'll give you the story of my life—and loves—after I finish a few sketches." She walked to a curtained closet and grabbed a hanger. She threw it at him. "Here; I wouldn't want your clothes to get creased."

Mike's eyes narrowed in a puzzled frown. "Are you always so grumpy in the morning?" As he asked her the question, he undid the buttons of his shirt. Standing around naked while Stacy sat across the room sketching him was not going to be easy. In fact, he cursed himself for ever having agreed to this ridiculous deal. But Stacy's taunting glare sparked his nerve. He slipped off his shirt, tossing it and the hanger onto a stool.

As he started undoing his belt, he looked up at Stacy. She sat poised on a stool a few feet away, sketch pad in hand. She gave him a brief, innocent smile and then pretended a preoccupation with her pad and pencils. However, Mike hadn't missed the still-taunting gleam in her eye or the glance of appreciation she'd given him before she'd averted her gaze.

As she drew a few preliminary lines on the paper, she said dryly, "Just keep in mind that this is strictly professional. There's really no need at all to feel embarrassed."

Damn her, he thought, she's really getting her kicks out of this whole thing. He had been about to ask her whether most models at least got to wear a pair of briefs. He changed his mind. If she wanted to challenge him, he wasn't going to back off. Why she was doing this, he couldn't figure out. But this was not the time to ponder that one. With as much nonchalance as he could muster, he slipped off his slacks and jockey shorts. He felt ridiculous, but he was determined not to give her any hint of his discomfort.

He met Stacy's gaze head on. She burst out laughing.

"Do you mind telling me what the hell is so funny?" he snarled. "Most women have quite a different reaction when they see me nude." He was enraged, and if he hadn't felt so utterly vulnerable, he would have walked over and shaken her soundly. As it was, he stood there trying to figure out where to put his hands.

Stacy tried to stop laughing. "I'm—I'm sorry," she sputtered between giggles. "It's just—you look so—silly standing there with nothing but your socks on."

Mike looked down at his feet. In his agitation and

rush to get the whole thing over with, he had completely forgotten about the brown socks that came almost up to his knees. He had to admit it was a comical picture. However, he was in no laughing mood.

He leaned against the stool and took them off. "Shall we get on with it," he muttered. This day would definitely go down as one of his more miserable ones, and it was still only morning.

"Sorry," she repeated. Her laughter had stopped; she was beginning to feel bad for Mike. His discomfort was obvious, and Stacy now felt a pang of regret. Clearing her throat, she tried to establish a strictly professional approach. She walked over to Mike and explained the pose she wanted him to take. He seemed to be having trouble following her directions.

Stacy hesitated. Standing next to him, she was disconcerted by her own responses. He had as magnificent a body as she had fantasized, and she was again acutely aware of his potent appeal. Mike was quick to pick up her discomfort now.

"I don't think I'm getting what you want me to do. Maybe you'd better help me." He echoed the innocent tone she had used on him earlier.

The tables had most definitely turned. Mike might have been the one standing there naked, but Stacy was the one feeling totally exposed.

"Or maybe," he said, "you're having second thoughts about using me as your model."

It wasn't so much the seductive challenge of his

words as it was that infuriatingly provocative grin of his that helped Stacy regain control. She matched his smile.

"Absolutely not. I think you're perfect."

"Why thanks, English. I was worried there for a minute that you were beginning to take me for granted. After all, seeing so many naked male models has to make you a little jaded."

He had stepped closer to her as he was speaking. Stacy wanted to move away, but she forced herself to hold her ground. If she gave in now, the battle would be lost. It was getting harder and harder to reclaim her anger or her resolve not to get intimately involved with Mike. Even though he continued to goad her, she could not ignore the intensely sensual air that enveloped them. If she let down her guard now, she was sure Mike would too. She reminded herself that she had worked with male models often enough without any problems. Then again, none of them had ever provoked these kinds of responses.

"Let your hand rest lightly on your hip," she explained, forcing herself to place his hand correctly. "And then keep your other hand relaxed at your side." She tried not to pay attention to the icy feel of her fingertips against Mike's warm skin. "Just take a small step forward . . . right. Okay, now tilt your chin up just an inch. Great." Mike complied with her wishes, thankfully keeping quiet. Her voice must have dropped a good octave or two, but there was no help for it. She was determined to carry off this scenario as planned.

Going back to her stool, she studied Mike critically. Holding the pose perfectly, he captured the very essence of the sculptured nude she wanted to create. She sketched with fast, efficient strokes, moving to a new position after each drawing. She had gone almost halfway around him when Mike broke the silence.

"Don't you ever give your models time off for good behavior?"

Stacy had been so absorbed she had lost track of time. "Sure, just let me finish this one sketch." After another couple of minutes she flipped the pad closed. "Okay, time off."

Mike stretched languidly. The early feelings of discomfort had disappeared. Stacy, too, had relaxed. She threw a towel from a shelf over to Mike, who casually placed it around his hips.

"How about something to drink?" Stacy was already pouring herself a cup of coffee.

"I have a better idea. How about something to eat? Say, like steak, toast, eggs, maybe some pancakes on the side."

"Slow down. I don't usually provide my models with meals."

"What services do you provide?" he quipped, lazily strolling to her worktable and flipping open the sketch pad.

"Will you please stop doing that," she said, walking over to him as he started turning the pages. She wasn't referring to his study of her sketches.

Mike understood perfectly what she was referring to.

"I might say the same to you," he said, stopping at one of the drawings to look at her carefully. "Why the sudden switch? Last night I thought we had . . ."

"Yes, tell me about last night," she challenged.

"Last night I did something I can't remember doing before. I told a woman I wanted her like crazy and then I turned around and walked out. Don't get me wrong. It wasn't a selfless act. I was out to save my skin. I really could fall for you, Stacy English. I think you could fall for me. That would leave us both out on a very big limb."

"I thought last night we agreed we could handle things without getting entangled," she said softly. "We were going to be on our best behavior, remember?"

"Stacy," he murmured, lightly caressing her shoulders, "I'm not very good at behaving myself. Especially standing around here with you, naked as a jaybird."

Mike's towel in no way blunted the impact of his virile presence. His hands slipped around to her back, and his eyes held hers in a persuasive gaze. "Aren't we asking an awful lot of ourselves?"

Stacy struggled to find her voice. "Mike, stop." She backed up, almost stumbling. "I—I don't want to go out on that limb." Gathering conviction as she moved farther away, she said, "It's not only an issue of sex. Maybe my resistance wouldn't hold out if that was all that we were dealing with. In two weeks you'll be gone." She curled her lips in a rueful grin. "And I don't work well when I'm hurting."

"Joe was wrong," Mike said, looking at her critically. "He told me this morning, when I tried to get out before the going got rougher, that if I could handle world disasters I could cope with you. Right now World War Three would be a picnic to cover by comparison," he teased, his smile tender and caressing.

"How about making it easier on both of us and getting dressed. I'll make you that breakfast."

She turned away quickly, knowing that if he touched her now, the meal would never materialize.

CHAPTER FOUR

Mike sat beside Stacy at the long conference table. There were only three other people present, giving the room a decidedly hollow feeling. Everyone but Mike was intent on the unrolled sheets of drawings sprawled across the top of the table. A small, extremely thin man in designer blue jeans and a different name designer's T-shirt was talking in an annoying, high-pitched voice. As Mike glanced at Stacy, he saw that she looked even more irritated than he felt. However, he guessed that her reaction had more to do with what the scrawny guy was saying than with his whiny sound. His observation proved accurate.

"This is completely asinine. I thought we were meeting to plan the dedication ceremony for my sculpture. Derek obviously thinks we're organizing a three-ring circus." Stacy's tone was icily deprecating.

She looked directly down the table at a distinguished-looking middle-aged gentleman dressed in a formal summer suit with tie despite the almost-one-hundred-degree temperature outside and the half-hearted air conditioning system inside. The man looked cool and complacent except for a slight creeping redness rising above his collar. Before he could respond to Stacy, Derek stood up and slammed his bony hand down on the table, his flushed face leaving no doubt as to how hot he was feeling.

He tugged on his tight-fitting T-shirt as he spoke. "I was hired to make this—this thing an event, not some tediously dull unveiling of a piece of stone."

Stacy flinched noticeably at his reference to her sculpture but she kept still.

"My understanding, Mr. Bennett, is that you wanted to draw a crowd, make this into something the city would talk about for weeks." He, too, stared at the well-dressed businessman as if expecting some support. "I have never had any of my dramatic events called a—a three-ring circus," he said, glaring at Stacy. Stacy's cool stare and slight smile clearly infuriated Derek, who tugged harder at the V neck of his shirt.

Mike glanced around the table. The third fellow in the room, a younger version of Mr. Bennett, with the same slick, well-groomed appearance, sat quietly taking notes. As Derek paused for air, only the sound of the secretary's pen scratching away at the pad filled the room.

Mr. Bennett cleared his throat. "Surely we can come up with a reasonable compromise."

Definitely a politician, Mike thought and smiled to himself.

"Now look, folks"—he swept his eyes from Stacy to Derek and back again to Stacy—"the mayor feels this is a very important occasion. Miss English's sculpture"—his eyes quickly shot down to his notes —"aptly called *Peace and Harmony*, represents something very meaningful to the entire city. The mayor wants the very message of peace and harmony to be—well, let's say he wants it to be our city's heartfelt motto . . ."

Mr. Bennett droned on for several more minutes, all about what the mayor wanted, what Stacy and Derek wanted, and what everyone in the city wanted. Mike could tell that neither Stacy nor Derek was listening. Both sat quietly staring at the table, more than likely preparing their arguments. Only the dapper young secretary seemed involved, his hand busily skimming across the page. Mike knew Bennett wanted to make sure the mayor, if he ever bothered to read the minutes of this meeting (which Mike seriously doubted), would have to commend his spokesman's efforts. When Bennett finally finished, Derek rushed to speak.

"Compromise is certainly not something I oppose, believe me. I am only interested in giving the mayor something he will be proud of. We might, I suppose, cut some of the musical numbers. I'll even forego the jugglers, since Miss English must be referring to them when she calls my event a circus. But I will emphasize again that they were part of my idea for amusing the children, who will not be quite as interested in the grand unveiling as the adults." Now it was his turn to cast his eyes down at Stacy with airy superiority.

"Mr. Bennett," Stacy said as she again focused her eyes on the official. She was completely poised and relaxed as she addressed him. "I was commissioned to do a meaningful and important sculpture. From my earlier talks with Mayor Wiener, I believe I have achieved my goal and have created a work of art that both he and the city can be proud of. That, I will again emphasize, is the point of the event—both to dedicate the sculpture and to publicize the message it represents. Now, if you plan an event around the dedication that fits the mood and the seriousness of the occasion, I will be only too happy to be present and accept the mayor's thanks. If, however, you approve this spectacle, I don't feel that I can attend." As she spoke she gathered up the few papers she had brought along. Standing, she added, "I do hope I've made myself clear. Now why don't I leave you to talk this all over, and then you can let me know your decision." As she turned toward the door, with Mike right behind her, she glanced back for a moment. "I am quite busy now on a new 'piece of stone,' so I advise you to let me know what the ceremony is going to be like as soon as possible." She glided out the door then, as Mike cast a wide smile back at the silent group before he followed her out.

Once on the street, Stacy's fast pace made Mike realize she was far more worked up than she had seemed at the meeting. Grabbing hold of her arm, he slowed her down a bit. She was muttering curses like a truck driver. Mike laughed. "You are a tough broad, English. Remind me always to stay on your side of the fence."

"Derek Morgan has got to be the biggest—"

"Please, English, my virgin ears," he said with a grin.

Stacy looked at Mike, paying attention to him for the first time since the meeting had started. "You're right." She nodded, although Mike was baffled about just what she was referring to. "Why should I lower myself to that—that ridiculously poor excuse for a—an organizer. Jugglers!" She said the word as if it was her choicest curse word by far.

"I have to admit," Mike said, his hand patting her back, "you handled that little group back there like a real pro."

"I am a pro," she snapped, ready to bite Mike's head off, too, if necessary.

"Whoa, I'm on your side, remember."

"Are you?" She tilted her head slightly and gazed steadily into his eyes.

"More and more, English. More and more." His

eyes held hers for a moment, the meaning of his words settling in for both of them. Then he recaptured his wry grin. "Beautiful, talented, and now I discover you're an absolute wonder with words. You've got it all. I'm definitely on the winning side."

"I'm hungry," Stacy announced suddenly, veering left toward a small storefront deli. "I'm going to drown my memories of this morning's farce in a cream soda and a large hot corned beef sandwich." There was no question of whether Mike planned to come along or not. Stacy, he was learning rapidly, was a woman with a mind of her own. Mike opened the door to the restaurant for her.

When Stacy finished giving the waitress her order, Mike told the moderately disheveled older woman to give him the same thing.

"I guess this isn't the best time to start my interview," Mike said with a slight smile.

"Why not," Stacy answered. "I'm perfectly fine." She shot him a quick grin. "Now that my corned beef sandwich is on the way."

"So you've got terrific recuperative powers, besides all your other great attributes. Okay, then tell me all the nitty-gritty details so I can write that profile on the true Stacy English. Let's give the readers something to read about."

"Where do you want me to begin?"

"You decide."

After a thoughtful pause, Stacy began. "I was born twenty-seven years ago, in a smart New York hospital, of course, where Mother claims I screamed continuously, much to her consternation. As their precious only child, I was not exactly what either of my parents had bargained for. My father admitted to me a long time ago that I was a disappointing baby. My thick black infant hair fell out quickly, and the little blond wisps that replaced it were slow in coming. My mother supposedly kept a cap on my head for the first ten months of my life, all of which time, they both claim, I spent bald and bawling." She paused as the waitress nearly dropped their sandwiches in front of them.

"How do I sound so far?" she asked before taking a large bite of the corned beef that was precariously hanging out of the seeded rye bread.

"You sure have improved over the years—at least where that blond mop of yours is concerned. As for the bawling, I'll have to withhold my judgment for a while."

Stacy laughed, wiping the greasy juice off her chin. "My lungs have improved over the years, and I can scream to tear the walls down when necessary."

"When is it necessary?" he asked.

"Whenever I don't get what I want, of course," she said cheerfully. "I was raised to be a spoiled brat who was always given what I wanted. So I've merely been trained over the years to keep expecting the same treatment." Her tone was happily facetious, but Mike realized that in some ways she was right. Her upbringing must have been an asset in helping

71

her carry off her demands at that meeting this morning. However, he also believed that Stacy was far from being a spoiled brat. She might be strong, tenacious and stubborn as the devil, but she also impressed him as a woman of integrity and warmth, the latter quality apparent despite her pretense at cool toughness. She had, in his assessment, earned the right to ask for respect as well as a lot of other things.

"Let's skip over the early years for a minute. I'm eagerly awaiting those promised juicy tidbits about your love life. Now that's something our readers love to read about. Which one of those fabulously eligible young men you are always flitting around with is on top of your list?" He tried to sound flip and casual, but his moist palms belied his light manner. It disturbed him to think about Stacy with any of those sophisticated, well-schooled, wealthy men. It also disturbed him that he found his thoughts disturbing!

Stacy looked at him for a moment, trying to gauge the meaning behind his words. Shrugging slightly, she said, "None of them is on top of my list, Mike. I don't have a list. I'm not interested in a single one of them. I'm not only spoiled, I'm infuriatingly picky. Most men bore me. I'm afraid I lied to you about that. I really don't have a lot of juicy tidbits. No wild romantic escapades, no funny, sexy little stories. I misled you, Mike. I'm a dull, hardworking artist. Most of my nights are spent with stone and chisel, not with one of the eligible young men who escort me around town. You're the first guy who's set my heart fluttering in a long time."

Mike found himself suddenly tongue-tied. She had zeroed right in on the real issue, and he wanted desperately to skirt it.

"Maybe we'd better go back to your childhood after all," he said, trying unsuccessfully to smile nonchalantly.

Stacy shrugged again. "Whatever you say. You're the reporter. Although you have picked my least favorite period."

"How come?" Mike asked, thankful that she hadn't pursued the topic of their relationship.

"I was not a very happy kid. Oh, I had the best care any well-bred little girl could ask for. Only most of it came from the various assortment of nannies, cooks and housekeepers who passed through our Fifth Avenue penthouse. I never could figure out the reasons any particular one came or went. From my child's-eye vantage point, it seemed to me that Mother simply grew bored of having the same servants around all the time. Now that I'm older and wiser, it has dawned on me that my parents were both exceedingly private people and whenever anyone, even an employee, penetrated too close or started to seem indispensable, they fired them and hired somebody new, who couldn't presume any type of relationship. I suppose that's why they sent me off to boarding school shortly after I was old enough to begin making demands for the kind of affection they were totally unable to give. Poor little rich girl, huh?" She made no pretense of a smile.

"Sounds lonely and sad to me."

"It was. I never seemed to find a comfortable niche for myself, at home or at school. Years before I was declared artistically eccentric and thereby acceptable, I was always considered slightly odd. While all my classmates gleefully showed off the lavish gifts their parents sent them at school, I used to either stuff my folks' bribes under the bed or give them away. I spent a lot of nights crying myself to sleep, concluding that I must have been an orphan my rich, successful parents adopted only to discover they had made a disastrous choice. But I'm their flesh and blood all right. My mother takes great delight out of my resemblance to her, and especially out of the endless comments about how she could easily pass for my older sister rather than my mother."

Mike could see the hurt and pain behind Stacy's large brown eyes—the delicately lovely little girl hidden inside the woman, yearning to belong, to feel cared for. He wanted nothing more than to sweep her up in his arms and lavish all the love on her that she had missed for so long.

Stacy stared blankly at her half-eaten sandwich. "I'm not feeling very hungry anymore. Sorry about my woeful tale. I don't usually go on about myself like that. And I didn't mean to make my folks out to be ogres. They're really a very generous, charming, bright couple. They simply have never been the type of people to show much affection or great interest in anything that doesn't fit into their carefully structured world. They gave up on me years ago, which has actually made my life easier and even made my relationship with them better. I like them a great deal more now that they've stopped putting so much effort into trying to mold me into a carbon copy of themselves—something I could never be. We may not be the closest of families, but we manage to do pretty well." She took a long drink of her soda and then said, "What about you? What was the Great Gallotti like as a little boy?"

"Let's just say I had no opportunity to be a spoiled kid. There wasn't enough money around to spoil me."

"Money isn't the only means of spoiling a kid," Stacy contended, irritated by Mike's snappy and sarcastic response.

"I thought I was the one doing the interview. It's your profile we're focusing on, not mine," Mike said stiffly. He had no intention of sharing his early years with Stacy, of telling her about his childhood on the other side of the tracks, in a world as foreign to hers as the planet Jupiter. Maybe she had ached for some attention and love, but she certainly knew nothing about real hunger. He had spent his childhood years watching his folks anxiously make out the monthly bills, always trying to figure out which ones could keep for another month. His parents had had to decide what they could do without every time Mike or one of his four brothers and sisters needed something for school. His life had not consisted of lavish presents, bribes or otherwise, and as a kid, he was lucky to get something other than a new pair of pants or a shirt when his birthday rolled around. He had his own sad little tale to tell, only he had no desire to tell it.

Stacy resented Mike's unwillingness to speak of himself. She had spilled out feelings she rarely discussed with anyone, and when she had tried to get him to open up a little about himself, he had slammed the door in her face. She didn't realize he was ashamed of his past. She saw his guardedness as an unwillingness to share, a desire to keep her from getting too close. His tactics were different from those of her parents, but when it came down to bare truth, the effect was the same. Well, she told herself, she had learned not to let her parents' remoteness bother her. She could damn well do the same with Mike.

She stood up abruptly, reached into her purse for some money, plunked it on the table next to the check and started for the door.

Her anger was unmistakable, and Mike knew he had hurt her by his defensive maneuvers. He caught up with her at the door.

"Sorry," he said, catching hold of the door before it smacked into him.

"Don't be," Stacy said coolly. "You aren't required to dish out your life story. It is certainly not part of your assignment."

"I wasn't considering my assignment while you were talking about yourself. I was thinking about you and what it must have been like to grow up in such a cold, unloving environment."

"I'm not looking for your pity. Anyway, I'm surprised you haven't come up with any snide asides. I couldn't ever match, I'm sure, the kind of hard knocks you were dealt—whatever they might be."

"Ouch. You have a powerful aim, English." He pretended a direct hit to the jaw.

Stacy's pace was even faster than when she had walked out of the meeting. This time when Mike grabbed her arm he forced her to a complete halt.

"Stacy, I don't want to fight with you. I really do feel bad for the way you were treated as a child. Take my word or not, I'm being open and honest with you."

"I don't think you know what openness is, Mike." Her words were biting, but her tone was tinged with sadness.

"Maybe so. I don't go around being open with many people any more than you normally go around baring your childhood scars."

"But I did bare them to you," Stacy said pointedly.

"I know," Mike said, finding nothing more he could say. Too many feelings had been stirred up inside him.

"Let's drop it," Stacy responded, seeing that Mike really was feeling troubled. Even though she still minded that he was so closed, deep down she also understood it.

That evening Mike once again dressed in his black jacket and bow tie, and he and Stacy attended a benefit dance. Mike kept forgetting exactly what the benefit was for, but he assumed it was a worthy cause or Stacy probably would not have bothered to come. She looked almost as bored as he felt during the seemingly endless dinner. With dessert came an equally endless seeming series of speeches, refreshing Mike's memory that this tedious event was a benefit for an arts camp for underprivileged youth. A worthy enough cause, he thought, but the kids would probably have made out better had these esteemed and wealthy people put the money they had spent on the furs and jewels they wore tonight toward the camp and skipped the pretentious ball.

He felt better when the dancing began. Stacy fit against him perfectly as they glided across the floor. She was dressed in a simple but elegant black silk gown. Its deep, rounded neckline contrasted enticingly with its soft, full-flowing sleeves. The gown tapered gently to her slim waist and then fell around her body down to her ankles. She not only looked fabulous, she felt terrific in his arms as they danced to a melodic old Count Basie tune.

Stacy had been very quiet all evening. As they

danced, Mike could sense tension in her body despite the fact that she followed him beautifully and easily.

"You're not still mad about today, are you?" he whispered against her ear.

Stacy pulled her head back to look up at him. "That dumb meeting? I haven't given it another thought. They'll come around by tomorrow, I guarantee you."

"I wasn't talking about the meeting for the dedication. I was referring to our encounter over corned beef afterward."

"Oh, that." Stacy took a few more steps before saying anything else. She had thought she'd forgotten her anger at Mike's refusal to talk about himself today. But she had to admit to herself that she still felt on edge. Being in his arms was not helping matters any. It felt both good and unnerving to be pressed against him. He was a good dancer, with just that right touch of sensuality to his movements. She kept having to fight off her lurking desire to do more than dance with him. When he had been so closed about his past this afternoon, it had reminded her of their agreement to keep things between them purely professional. She had obviously not kept her part of the bargain this afternoon. Mike, however, seemed to have no trouble at all keeping his distance. When she had started talking about herself, it was because she had felt a need to have Mike understand her better. She had wanted to share something with him. Maybe, she decided, it wasn't so much his silence about his own background that had gotten to her. Maybe it had more to do with her having forgotten that Mike was merely doing his job by digging into her past.

She did not like being deceitful, but she also had no intention of putting herself on the line again.

"I'm not angry at you, Mike. I guess bringing up old stuff can rekindle some not-so-pleasant memories. Some things are better left unsaid," she commented innocently, but when Mike gave her a deep, questioning look, she added, "I'm sure you of all people would agree with that."

Damn him, why did he always get her to say more than she wanted. Now he grinned openly. "You are masterful at a hell of a lot of things, English, but you are a lousy actress."

"That, Gallotti, was one example of something better left unsaid."

They both laughed, and it helped to clear the air. They were beginning to relax more, and at the end of the dance Mike held her to him a few moments after the music faded. Stacy didn't protest.

As they mingled among the large group of people attending the benefit, Mike was frequently recognized. Stacy was surprised and impressed by how well known and highly respected he was. Several people got into lengthy discussions with him about various newsworthy issues. And Stacy noticed that more than a few women showed a particularly avid interest in Mike, an interest that clearly had little to do with what he wrote about. Stacy alternated between feeling intensely jealous and telling herself that she had no business feeling anything for Mike at all. After all, she thought, she and Mike were not involved in a personal way. Eventually, however, Stacy gave up attempting to convince herself. She settled for trying to shrug off her irritation at the women who flocked around.

Back on the dance floor, Mike was as lively and cheerful as Stacy was morose. He obviously thrived on attention, and Stacy decided that he had played up his sexual magnetism tonight to his greatest advantage. Well, she forced herself to conclude, why not? He's brilliant, successful and incredibly good-looking. He had every right to play up his assets. Again she reminded herself that there was nothing between them and that was the way they both wanted it. She tried hard to act casually and engage in some light banter as they danced. Not succeeding too well, she was greatly relieved when an old friend, Charlie Hitchcock, cut in for a dance. She cheerfully swung around into Charlie's arms, getting a small degree of pleasure from Mike's annoyed expression as he watched her new dance partner whisk her away. Before Mike could step off the floor, a strikingly attractive brunette approached him, asking him to dance. After the number Stacy and Charlie joined Mike and his new friend.

"Stacy, you never told me you knew the celebrated Mike Gallotti," the brunette gushed, clinging to

Mike's arm in just the right way to make her ample cleavage in her low-cut gown even more pronounced. Stacy caught Mike's interested gaze. From the way Cynthia Walters smiled up at him, Stacy could tell she was delighted by his blatant admiration.

"Sorry, Cynthia," Stacy said, angry at the stilted sound of her voice. "Mr. Gallotti, meet Cynthia Walters. Although I gather the two of you are already getting acquainted. Mike is doing a story on me for the *Globe.*"

"Oh," Cynthia said, continuing to cling to her newfound possession. "Then there isn't anything romantic going on."

"Purely business," Stacy answered, inwardly fuming as Mike kept his eyes focused on Cynthia's enticing breasts.

"Then you won't mind if I kidnap him for a little while. It's such a marvelous treat to get a chance to hear firsthand about all those exciting news events Mike has covered."

Stacy was well aware that news was the furthest thing from Cynthia's mind, but Mike was grinning with pleasure at Cynthia's gushing interest. News obviously wasn't the most important thing on his mind either.

"He's all yours, Cynthia," Stacy said blandly. "Only don't expect to get too much out of him. You might be disappointed by what he has to say."

"Oh, I doubt that anything Mike might say would be disappointing."

Stacy whirled around to Charlie, who was oblivious to the hostile undercurrent in the conversation. She didn't miss Mike's sexy little laugh as she said to her partner, "Come on, Charlie, they're playing our song."

Ten minutes later, with Mike and Cynthia still cozily dancing, Stacy pleaded a headache and asked Charlie to take her home.

CHAPTER FIVE

Stacy's headache grew painfully real during the ride home. She was content to let Charlie do most of the talking while she contributed only a few "aha's" and "really's" at appropriate moments. She was relieved when he was unable to find a parking space and had to let her out in front of her building. She gave him a quick peck on the cheek and thanked him for the ride.

When she stepped into her apartment after what felt like an interminable wait for the creaky elevator, she walked directly to the sofa and collapsed on it, her arm swinging across her forehead to try to ease the steady, painful pounding.

This business with Mike was slowly but surely undoing her. She had experienced a wider range of disturbing emotions during these two days than she had in a very long time. And now to top it all off—jealousy. There was no skirting the reality. Seeing Mike and Cynthia in their snug little embrace had produced the pulsating ache in her head, and her fantasies of Mike and the voluptuous Ms. Walters going off together for the night were now causing a full-scale migraine.

Why did she have to find him so damned attractive? Why did Mike Gallotti fit every woman's bill of the ideal man? He was downright universal, the louse. Ranting was not helping her headache any, but it did make her feel a drop of emotional relief. She eased herself into an upright position, paused for a few minutes to calm the increased pounding and finally slowly stood up and walked into the bathroom for some aspirin. Catching her reflection in the mirror, she groaned. Jealousy was definitely not doing her looks any good. Just as she was vowing to get those ruinous feelings under control, she heard a loud banging at the door. The pounding on the wood started the pounding in her head all over again.

"Stop," she screamed out, both palms pressed against her temples. Who the hell could it be at this ungodly hour? Mike's bellowing voice immediately answered her question.

"Damnit, then open this door," he growled.

Stacy inched over to the door, keeping her hands at her head. When she got there she half leaned against the cool wood. "Go away, Mike. I'm about to go to bed."

"I'm not going anywhere until you tell me why you ran out on me."

"You seemed happily occupied, and I felt like coming home. It seems to me we both made out just fine."

"Just fine, huh? You call leaving me in the clutches of that vulture just fine!"

Stacy grinned, forgetting her headache for a moment. She remembered it again quickly when he suddenly pounded on the door again.

"I don't like talking through wood. Will you open this door?"

"No. I'm tired and I want to go to sleep."

"Stacy, this is ridiculous. You know that. You have no reason to be jealous of Cynthia what's-her-name."

She didn't bother denying the obvious. Mike would not have needed ESP to figure out the reason for her adolescent flight. "I know," she said instead. "I've been stubborn, unreasonable, ridiculous, jealous—fill in any missing blanks. Now I'm going to go to bed and try to wake up tomorrow morning feeling like my old steady, practical self again." Pressing her elbow against the door, she righted herself and wearily started off to her room.

There was one more light rapping knock that stopped her movement. She stood still, waiting.

"Good night, English. Sweet dreams."

She smiled and listened as Mike's footsteps faded down the hall.

Mornings were Mike's best time. He always woke up feeling invigorated and energetic even if he had only gotten a couple of hours of sleep—as he had last night. He'd dreamed about Stacy for those few hours, and this morning his thoughts were still focused on her. Her honesty about her feelings last night had made a strong impact on him. She was a very special woman, the kind that came along once in a lifetime. Too bad, he thought, she showed up now. The timing was lousy. He was at the height of his career, one that he still firmly believed held no room for a serious relationship with a woman. His mind couldn't wander on his job, and as he had spelled out for Stacy from the start, he liked being footloose and free.

Still, he didn't try to fight the constant fantasies that filtered through his head as he hopped a cab over to her loft. He was eager to see her again, not even minding the idea of posing any longer. He was also beginning to talk himself into the idea of a brief affair. He could handle it, he lied to himself. He, like Stacy, was a rotten liar, but he did at times have a greater ability to deny reality. That, he thought, was probably why he was good at his job. If he ever gave too much thought to the dangers he constantly faced, he would probably run home and crawl under his covers.

When he got to Stacy's apartment, she was slow in coming to the door. He hoped, for both their sakes, that she was in a good mood, as Mike was not about to have another conversation through a closed door.

But Stacy opened it right away after asking who was there. At least she parted the door halfway, positioning herself in such a way as to bar his entry.

She looked freshly scrubbed and rested and as irresistible as ever.

"What's up? Am I being barred from work because I showed up late again?" he asked lightly.

"It isn't that," she said a little hesitantly. "I forgot to tell you last night—there was too much else going on—I won't need you to pose this morning. I'm working with a model who will be your fill-in after you leave."

"Oh." Mike made no effort to move.

"You've got the day off," she said a little awkwardly. "Most folks love time off from work."

"Well, posing is only half of my job. I'm still on assignment—two weeks in the life of Stacy English, Girl Wonder. I'll sit on the sidelines and watch you work. With my clothes on, I'll probably be a lot better able to concentrate on your style and technique." He grinned warmly, a distinctly amused sparkle in his hazel eyes.

Stacy reluctantly stepped back and let him in. She followed him in the direction of the studio.

An extremely attractive dark-haired young man, a

small white towel draped around his hips, was comfortably lounging in a director's chair. He glanced curiously at Mike and then stood up when he saw Stacy.

Mike had not really thought about the fact that the new model would be in the same state of undress as he had been when he had posed. This guy seemed much less uptight about it, slipping his towel languidly off his waist and returning to the raised platform. Mike couldn't decide whether he felt more uncomfortable posing or sitting and watching Stacy carefully position this sleek young hunk of a man. She seemed as natural and comfortable as the model. Before she returned to her sketching, she glanced over her shoulder at a slightly red-faced Mike and asked innocently, "You sure you won't be bored?"

Mike didn't bother answering. He was far from bored. He was embarrassed, uncomfortable and irritated. The relaxed intimacy between Stacy and the model was maddening to him. She had muttered a brief introduction when they'd come into the studio together, but Mike had been so thrown when he saw the six foot tall, nearly nude man that he didn't catch his name. Not that it mattered. The guy, and Stacy, were oblivious to Mike's presence. However, Mike was quick to spot that the two were not oblivious to each other. It seemed that each time Stacy walked over to the nude model to suggest a different pose, she always touched him. And, he decided, she made a hell of a lot more suggestions to this guy than she had made to him. She had given Mike the impression that only one pose was necessary. Now she was moving this man around like he was a dancer.

She was also warmly approving and enthusiastic about the model's poses and laughed easily with him when he made some clever little remark. Mike was sitting on a stool, becoming angrier by the second. Just how often did this guy model for her anyway? And maybe she didn't fool around with the wealthy bachelors she dated, but he had never asked her directly about her involvements with the men who worked for her. It was such a cozy setup, and one of them was already naked and ready for anything.

He was so caught up in his ruminations that he didn't hear Stacy when she called over her shoulder to him.

"What?"

"I asked you if you had any questions for me. These are just preliminary sketches, so I can give you some information while I work."

That's great, he told himself. And how am I supposed to concentrate on an interview when she's standing there busily admiring and drawing some naked man.

"I'm making some mental notes right now about the way you work," he muttered.

Stacy grinned. "I don't always work this way, of course. Some of my models lack the ability to give me what I want. When I get my hands on someone as talented as Zeke, it really inspires me." She turned back to her sketch pad, not needing to see Mike's hot glare. Her imagination was all that was necessary. She grinned again.

She had felt as awkward as Mike at first, having him sitting there behind her, watching Zeke and her. She really had meant to tell Mike yesterday not to come this morning. It was the only time over the next couple of weeks that Zeke was available, and she did have to make certain that he would be a suitable substitute for Mike. She had intentionally led Mike to believe that Zeke was more than ideal. The truth was, he in no way offered the magnetism and innate sensuality that Mike exuded. He was good and he would certainly do. But he would never come close to filling Mike's shoes.

It was after seeing Mike's discomfort this morning, as well as his surfacing touch of jealousy, that she had found herself milking the situation for all it was worth. She wanted him to see that she wasn't the only one who could get jealous and start imagining all kinds of ideas. Stacy was certain Mike was having more than his share of fantasies right now about her and Zeke. Of course, there was nothing between them. Zeke was merely a good model. In fact, he was happily married, going to law school at night and only modeling temporarily to put some food on the table until he passed the bar exam. She knew these were facts Mike would never guess.

Mike was about ready to clear out. The dose of jealousy he was giving himself was not helping his empty stomach. Coming here, he had imagined another delightful breakfast with Stacy, followed by some modeling and then whatever else happened. This scene definitely did not fit in with his plans.

Mike stood and stretched. Before he said anything, Stacy smiled at him. "I'm about done, so if you want to stay for lunch, we can get back to your interview. There's a frozen quiche in the fridge. Why don't you pop it into the oven for me?"

If she had invited Zeke to join them, Mike would have offered a speedy "no thank you, sweetheart" and made for the door. But she didn't say anything to her model, who was slipping into his tight-fitting jeans and telling her that he had to get to his next assignment and would see her in two weeks. Mike walked into the kitchen and threw the cheese pie into the oven.

Stacy came in a few minutes later. She went over to the cupboard and brought out a bottle of wine and a couple of glasses. She poured them each a drink, handing Mike one as he leaned against the sink.

"You are inspiring to watch when you are so inspired," he quipped.

"Thanks. I'm glad you enjoyed watching," she replied blithely. "Zeke does have all the necessary qualities, don't you think?" She smiled with just a touch of provocativeness.

"You're the artist, not me. With all your experience, I have no doubt you can spot the good ones right off the bat."

Stacy reached into the fridge for some lettuce, tomatoes and cucumbers. "Onion?" she asked, pulling one out of the bin.

"Why not? Unless you plan on doing some heavy necking."

Stacy put the onion on her cutting board and began slicing it.

"Ask away while I make up the salad." Stacy smiled, gently shoving him away from the sink so she could rinse off the vegetables. Mike only moved a few inches. She kept brushing against him as she ran the water over the greens.

"Let's get back to your love life. What you've given me so far is dull reading at best." Mike gave her a funny little smile.

"I always thought the *Globe* was a respectable paper, not some scandalous tabloid. I can't imagine Joe Turner printing anything racy."

"You can skip the intimate details, or else leave me to edit out what wouldn't be suitable material," Mike countered.

Stacy laughed. "Haven't we been over this stuff already? Those eligible bachelors who wine and dine me offer nothing you would need to edit."

"How about your models? Can you say the same for them?" His tone was now less teasing, and Stacy saw that his smile had vanished.

"I don't usually mix work and fun, Mike. You should know that already."

"I bet you've made some exceptions, though. Like

with someone as inspiring as Zeke. I would think any woman would be sorely tempted with a guy like that, even if he did happen to work for her."

"Why beat around the bush, Gallotti. Why not ask straight out if Zeke or any other of my great-looking models and I fool around after working hours?" Stacy's tone was no longer amused, either. She did not like Mike's insinuating tone. The jealousy bit was going too far.

"Okay, do you?"

"No."

"Try me again." He caught hold of her arm, swinging her around. "I know damn well you're not a twenty-seven-year-old virgin. So who does get between those bed sheets next to you if it isn't a model or one of your socialite beaux?"

She dropped the tomato on the floor and slapped him with all the strength that years of wielding a hammer had given her. Furious, Mike grabbed her and pushed her hard against the sink. The next minute he was pressing her against his own hard body, his mouth descending on hers, capturing her lips with a fierce possessiveness.

Stacy was fighting mad. She pounded on his chest, tried to squirm out of his vise-like grip and kept her lips firmly shut in outraged indignation.

When Mike loosened his grip slightly and tilted his head down to look at her, he grinned at the determined defiance in her eyes. He knew he had only to keep up his tactics and in another minute that defiance would be transformed into desire. He had already felt how her body trembled and her lips quivered despite her fury. But the idea of a battle of wills left him unsatisfied. He wanted Stacy very much, but he wanted her when she was truly ready. He had no taste for overpowering her, subduing her and conquering her. His fierce embrace had been the product of both his own insidious jealousy and his anger at himself that Stacy had begun to uncover so many long-buried emotions.

"Sorry, English. I guess I can be as ridiculous, unreasonable and jealous as you."

Stacy gave him a long, hard look before her features softened to the hint of a smile.

"Well, it just goes to prove even more how much alike we really are," she said, her smile widening. She was also aware that although Mike had loosened his steely grip, his arms were still holding her lightly. She did not make any objection.

"You do have a maddening effect on me," Mike said, drawing a deep breath. "I keep forgetting all our vows to behave. How about you?"

It was definitely not fair to ask her that question while at the same time he was nuzzling her neck and planting tiny, erotic kisses below her ear.

"What was that question again?" Stacy sighed as he found a particularly tantalizing spot near her throat. His hands began finding some wonderful places as well, strong fingers gently massaging her back, sliding up and down her spine. When he bent his head toward her this time, Stacy's was already tilted up to meet him.

There was no resistance now as his mouth sought her parted lips. Her arms slipped around his neck, her fingers tangling in his thick black curls. She received his exploring tongue hungrily, her whole body responding to the erotic foray.

Her back pressed hard against the edge of the sink but she was mindless of the pressure. She could focus on nothing but the all-consuming sensations that were coursing through her body as Mike's kisses grew deeper and more passionate. His body enveloped her and she felt a delicious sense of being swallowed by him. She returned his kisses with burning intensity, her soft moans the only sounds in the room.

"We do find the craziest places to neck, English," he whispered in her ear, his body still tightly pressing into hers. "In front of the Plaza, at the kitchen sink . . . How about being mundane for a change? Let's try the bedroom." All his vows to stay uninvolved with Stacy had long since disappeared. He didn't even care that this was likely to develop into something far more than an uncomplicated little affair. He had never felt this drawn to any woman, and he wanted her so much that all his fears were forgotten.

As soon as he spoke, Mike could feel Stacy pull back in his arms. His words seemed to break the spell. They gave her time to consider the consequences, weigh her decision. He decided as he looked into her questioning eyes that he should have taken her right there on the kitchen floor.

"Mike, I . . ."

"Stacy, I want to make love to you. I never was good at promising to behave myself. Look, everything we want has a price. I think that this is worth the price. I'm crazy about you, Stacy English. Why can't we just live in the present—have the joy of really being together while it lasts. It will be something precious we'll both always be able to remember." He knew no words were going to change her tense, watchful eyes. He was saying them for himself more than her.

"I want you, Mike. Right now my body feels like putty in your hands. If you swept me up in your arms and carried me off to the bedroom, I couldn't fight you. I wouldn't want to. I've been having fantasies of making love with you since you first stepped through that door. The only thing is, I can't guarantee I'll happily pay the price later. I can be very miserly. When I find something of value I don't easily let it go, even when it's in my own best interest. I told you I was a spoiled brat."

"I knew this was going to be a tough assignment," he said with a grin. He eased himself away from Stacy, inadvertently stepping directly on the tomato she had dropped on the floor. He looked down at the mess and groaned. What an insane scene—his body still bursting with hot, throbbing desire, his mind trying to reconcile his need with the reality of her refusal, and now this. He gazed at the pulpy red mass, splatterings of which now decorated the cuffs of his white chinos. Stacy, her own body still trembling, followed his gaze. Then they looked into each other's eyes and broke out laughing.

"Is this all part of the price I have to pay for wanting you, English?"

"It's only the beginning, Gallotti. I warned you."

Stacy picked up a sponge from the sink, bent down and scooped up the tomato. Her attempts at getting the red stains off Mike's pants, however, were far less successful. Eventually he told her to forget it, claiming he'd charge the cleaning bill to Joe Turner as hazardous duty costs.

They were still chuckling when they both smelled smoke. Stacy dashed to the stove. The bubbling cheese had oozed out of the tin pie plate onto the bottom of the oven and mixed with some earlier spatterings of oil. She quickly shut off the stove and pulled the quiche out. Luckily it was only a little overbrowned.

"Lunch?" She peered at him with baleful brown eyes. "It really is a good quiche—or at least it was until recently."

Mike laughed. For all the disasters that had just befallen them, his body had not settled down and lunch was the last thing he had on his mind.

"Thanks anyway, beautiful. But I think I've gone through enough dangers for one morning."

She sighed, setting the steaming pie down on the

counter. She was no longer interested in lunch, either. Mike gave her a light peck on the forehead and started for the door.

"Mike, maybe you want to skip tonight." They had planned to attend Sam Collins's latest showing at a local SoHo gallery. Stacy had told Mike a little about Sam, and Mike wanted to meet him, thinking he would provide some interesting side material for Stacy's profile.

"No, don't worry about me. I have marvelous recuperative powers." He may have been desperate to put some distance between himself and Stacy now but he knew that by tonight he would be aching to see her again. Besides, a crowded art gallery was safe territory. He refused to think about afterward, when he would take her back home.

The gallery was already quite filled by the time Stacy and Mike arrived. Sam Collins had established a reputation as one of the shining new comers in the art world. The price of his works, while reflecting the growth of his popularity, was still low enough to attract modest collectors as well as the more serious ones looking for surefire bargains.

The inevitable spread of cheeses, carafes of wine and plastic cups was stretched out along the top of a long table at the side of the gallery. A good number of people migrated to that area. Mike and Stacy each took a glass of wine and began to walk around to look at the paintings. Sam was busily talking with what looked like a serious buyer. Stacy smiled a greeting and then started to tell Mike about some of the background for Sam's works. She was familiar with all of them and explained to Mike that Sam's art was highly motivated by his perception of the environment. He took what he saw and interpreted it on canvas in his own inimitable, abstract expressionist style.

Mike had always preferred realistic paintings to the more obscure forms of art. But Sam's work was so dynamic and exciting, so vibrantly colorful and intense that Mike was completely taken with almost every one of Sam's canvases. Only a few, done in dark, somber tones, did not move him. One small work—Stacy had told him it was Sam's view of a subway station at rush hour—intrigued him enough to purchase it.

Stacy had not been aware of how much she had wanted Mike to like Sam's work. Now, feeling elated that he had actually decided to own one of her friend's paintings, she realized how important it had been to her. It was one more thing they shared—a link that bound them together. When Mike casually put his arm around her as they looked at one of Sam's paintings, she slipped her arm around his waist and rested against him, feeling closer to him than she had felt to anyone in a very long time.

Later Sam came over to them with Annie, and Stacy introduced everyone. Annie was thrilled to meet Mike, telling him quite openly that he was the sexiest reporter she had ever seen on TV and that he looked even better in person. Stacy laughed, not feeling at all threatened by her friend's overt admiration. For the first time Stacy really could see the strong and loving bond that existed between Sam and Annie. It was that thought that sparked an odd little twinge of jealousy.

A local art critic who had earlier bent Sam's ear now accosted Stacy, bustling her off to a corner to prattle on about the latest trends in modern art. She gave Mike a hopeless shrug, sipped at her wine and tried to pay attention to what the critic was saying.

"Stacy's really something, isn't she?" Sam said to Mike.

"Yep, she's something all right." They gave each other a knowing smile.

"I thought I'd be dead and buried before I ever saw that woman smitten," Sam remarked lightly, but Mike could see there was serious intent behind his words. "You do know she's crazy about you? Oh, she'll probably deny it down to the end, to herself as well as to you. But I'm something of an expert on Stacy English. To coin a phrase, I love her like a sister—a very treasured sister. I would never want to see her get hurt, you know what I mean?"

Sam's words were as much an expression of concern as a warning, and Mike found himself liking Sam as a man even more than he admired him as an artist.

"Stacy's a lucky lady to have a friend like you. It's

good to know she's got someone who cares looking out for her. I sure as hell wouldn't want to be the guy who hurts her. Besides, I happen to care about Stacy as much as you. Maybe more."

"I'm going to tell you something, then, Gallotti— between the two of us. The details are Stacy's own business. But specifics aside, let's just say that a long time ago Stacy thought she'd fallen in love. She was in Paris. She was young, innocent, impressionable— thought she'd found her true love and was going to live happily ever after. The only kink in the fairy tale was that the guy omitted telling his starry-eyed young love that he was already very much married. When she finally found out, she was devastated. Couldn't work for months. She told me the sad tale quite a while ago. It's the reason for her staying clear of intimate relationships. Her conclusion was that love and art don't mix. My conclusion is that she was so hurt she made up her mind never to expose herself to that kind of risk again. Her dedication to her sculpting became a useful excuse. At least that's how I read it. You can give it any interpretation you want. Only keep in mind, Stacy may be a lot older, wiser and more experienced now, but underneath she's still mighty vulnerable."

"Thanks, Sam. I will keep it all in mind. The truth of the matter is I sometimes feel pretty vulnerable myself. Stacy and I have decided we had both better protect ourselves for the time being."

"Well, pal, all I can say is good luck. It looks to

me as if you're both going to need all the luck you can get." He squeezed Mike's shoulder in a warm, friendly gesture. "One of these days I ought to give you my spiel on the beauty of love. But my guess is that you're probably as stubborn and scared as Stacy, and I'd be whistling Dixie."

Annie, who had gone off earlier to chat with some friends, came back then and slipped her arm lovingly around Sam. Sam bent and kissed her and, looking back at Mike, said, "You don't know what you're missing, my friend. There's nothing like a loving woman to come home to. Right, Annie old girl?"

"You bet, Sam."

Mike sighed, feeling a vague twinge of envy as he looked at the happy couple.

CHAPTER SIX

Mike should have felt proud of himself, but he didn't. During the last five days he had been on his best behavior, and Stacy had followed suit. She had even made things a little easier for both of them by continuing her sketches of Mike without asking him to undress. She claimed she'd done enough nude drawings. She wasn't kidding either of them, but Mike was not about to argue.

He had even managed to get enough information together to start writing the profile. Everything was going according to plan. And he had never felt more miserable. Stacy had not only crawled under his skin, she had lodged herself right in his heart, mind and soul. He was filled with thoughts of her and with a yearning desire that went beyond any purely physical need.

The worst part was that there was no way to come to terms with his dilemma. Time was racing by. In another week he would be on assignment in London, shortly after that the Middle East. After that he would probably be off to some other distant part of the world. He knew that if he was going to continue to function as a journalist, had to keep his wits about him, which meant somehow, some way getting rid of his perpetual desire for Stacy English.

Mike had hoped he would be able to work her out of his system. He hadn't succeeded.

He decided on his way to her loft this morning that it was time to confront their mutual problem. His instincts told him Stacy was feeling as miserable as he was and had been no more successful at eradicating her desire.

Had he ESP as well as good instincts, he would have known that Stacy's mind that morning was echoing all his thoughts, and her body echoed all his frustrated desires.

When Stacy sat down at the kitchen table and opened the mail, however, all thoughts of Mike evaporated. An artist friend from San Diego had sent her a clipping from an L.A. newspaper. When she finished reading it, she slammed her fist on the table, upsetting her cup of coffee. She was so angry she didn't bother to wipe it up. Storming out of the kitchen, she paced up and down the large loft until she heard a knock on her door.

"Who is it?"

"How many models are you expecting this morning?" Mike asked lightly.

Stacy stared at the closed door. "Oh."

"Oh?"

"Go away, Mike."

"Not that again. Why is it you take such pleasure out of keeping me behind locked doors? Is there some new crime I've committed that has slipped my mind?" His tone remained easy and amused.

"I'm—I'm sick. I'm taking the day off. I'll see you tomorrow, okay?" Her tone told Mike that something was definitely wrong.

"Of course it's not okay. What kind of sick? Can I do anything to help? Open up."

"No."

"Stacy . . ."

"I—I hate having people around when I'm sick. I just want to be left alone. It's nothing serious, honest. Probably a—a flu or something."

"I've got remedies for whatever ails you, my sweet, so open up. I'm just going to stand out here pounding away until you do. Staying cooped up alone in your loft all day isn't going to make you feel any—" The door swung open as Mike finished. "Better."

She stood glaring at him with the defiant expression he had come to know well. She was also paler than usual and looked drawn and upset.

"You really are sick," he said, stepping inside and shutting the door. He reached his hand out and pressed it to her forehead.

Just as he touched her, she burst into tears and ran to the couch. She threw herself across it, sobbing into the pillow. When Mike kneeled beside her, she turned her head away, mumbling something that he couldn't make out. He was getting more and more concerned.

"Come on, baby, tell me what it is." Names of fatal diseases flashed through his mind as a line of perspiration broke out across his brow.

All at once she sat bolt upright, her face set in an angry grimace. The tears, still drenching her cheeks, stopped as precipitously as they had begun. Now she was mumbling some choice curses under her breath.

"I sure as hell hope those descriptive remarks aren't meant for me," Mike said, sitting down beside her on the couch.

She glanced to the side, looking at him for a moment as though she'd forgotten he was there. "Oh, Mike, I told you to go home. I'm not fit for human company."

"Do you always get this mad when you're sick?"

"I'm not that kind of sick."

"I was beginning to get that message."

She stood up and walked into the kitchen. A moment later she came out and returned to the couch.

She handed Mike the newspaper clipping without a word.

She began pacing again while he read it.

"I see what's ailing you," Mike said, setting the clipping on the coffee table.

"Can you believe the gall? That critic has as much insight into my work as—as . . ."

"As you thought I was going to have?"

"You're an ace connoisseur compared to this nincompoop. And did you catch those snide innuendoes about my having moved beyond my capabilities? And that as decorations for buildings my work had some merit, but that he could not agree with those critics who hail my sculpture as art. That I try to compensate for my missing skill by working in such large proportions; that—that—"

"I read every last word, Stacy. Come here and sit down."

"No. I don't want to sit. I want to hop a plane for L.A. and punch that overblown windbag in the nose. I want to take him and—and . . ."

She strode over to the couch and sat down heavily. Mike put his arm around her. Again, his touch seemed to spark a flood of tears. This time she didn't pull away. She sobbed into Mike's chest, letting him cradle her in his arms.

"The guy is a dolt, sweetheart. Compared to all the rave reviews you must have amassed, this can't matter. Anyone who knows anything about art knows you're fantastically talented, skilled, imaginative."

Stacy rubbed at her eyes with the palms of her hands. She sat up and gave Mike a weak smile. He brushed away a few of her tears, too, and went on. "Even I know how good you are—and you know my credentials. Only an idiot or someone out to get himself noticed would write a review like that. It isn't even written well. And on that I *am* an expert."

"I know. I know I'm overreacting."

His grin indicated that that was an understatement. She laughed, but her frown quickly reappeared.

"You might as well make a note, Gallotti, that I'm lousy at taking criticism—especially the undeserved kind. It kind of makes me see red."

"Red? Sweetheart, you go totally Technicolor," he said, but his eyes held hers in warm understanding.

"It's just that I need to feel in control of things. When some jerk—in L.A. yet—writes something from left field about me and there is really nothing I can do about it, I feel so helpless. I've worked damn hard at what I do; believe in the beauty and artistic merit of my sculptures. I'm good, Mike, really good. And you're right—plenty of critics, ones I truly respect—have given me my due. So why do I have to fall apart over one lousy clipping?"

"How did you get hold of it, anyway?"

"A friend—and I use that term advisedly—sent it to me. A struggling artist, of course. Probably wanted to remind me what it's like to suffer through bad reviews."

"Nice friend!"

"It worked, too. I'm suffering, all right." She got up and started pacing again.

"Stacy, settle down. You already agreed it isn't the end of the world."

Stacy came to a halt, turning only her head to stare at him. "I know that. I said so myself. I don't need any pat utterings from you, pal."

"Hold it there, English." Mike stood up and walked up to her. "Don't go biting my head off now because there's no other one available."

"Look, I'm sorry, okay? But I did tell you to go away. I've got to get this out of my system. This is how I do it. I scream, I rant, I cry, I pace and then I start all over again."

"Until?"

"Until I either get laryngitis or—or trip over the carpet and break my neck." She grinned and looked him straight in the eye. "What is it about you, Gallotti, that always makes me end up laughing no matter how mad I get?"

Mike grinned back. "I'm not sure. Maybe it's the way I wear my socks. You probably start picturing me standing around dressed in my birthday suit and brown argyles and just can't keep yourself from cracking up."

Stacy laughed harder at Mike's reminder of his first modeling session. "Oh, Mike, what am I going to do with you?" With a delicate motion she reached up and stroked his cheek.

"I could give you a very appealing answer to that question." He smiled, a provocative twinkle in his eyes.

"Damn you, Mike," she murmured. "You are not only gorgeous, talented and funny—you've got to turn out to be caring and sensitive as well. How am I supposed to keep resisting you?"

"I guess it's going to be impossible."

"But neither of us can afford any serious entanglement, right?" Her voice lacked conviction.

"Right." Mike nodded. His voice held less.

"And if we start—getting more intimate—we're going to be getting in over our heads . . ."

"Way over," he agreed matter-of-factly as he started to toy with a lock of her hair.

"I'm going to start missing the stone and bashing my thumbs, and you're going to forget to duck one day because you'll be having hot thoughts about my body . . ."

"Very dangerous," he agreed, caressing her cheek, then slipping down to her neck and shoulders.

"Exactly," she half sighed, half murmured, trying to ignore the sexy little indentation in the center of his chin. "We have to stay rational, right?"

"Wrong." He grinned. "I haven't had a rational thought in my head since I set eyes on you."

"This is not the way this conversation should go. You're supposed to support me, back my faltering determination. Why aren't you racing out of here? Isn't that ticker of yours fluttering? Mine's going like crazy, Mike."

She took a step backward. Mike reached out for her.

"And you accused me of talking too much. Come here, English. I want you to feel my fluttering heart."

She moved toward him, letting him place her hand on his heart.

"It's fluttering all right," she whispered.

"I want you, Stacy. There's just no more running away from it." He took her in his arms, bent over and kissed her tenderly on the lips, then backed off slightly to look down at her.

"I've been filled with fantasies about you since I first set eyes on you. I want to make them real," she whispered breathlessly.

They lay together on the large platform bed, the huge skylight overhead bathing them in the warmth of the sun.

Impatient to cast aside all barriers, they had taken off their clothes as they walked across the loft, leaving a trail of garments along the floor. There was no hesitation, no doubt, no tension as Mike scooped her into his arms a few feet from the bed and lovingly placed her on the sheets. Stacy wound her arms around his neck, pulling him down on top of her.

He rolled over to his side, afraid of crushing her. She seemed so small and fragile, so delicately beautiful. Still clinging to him, she moved with him so that now they lay together side by side. Stacy reveled in the feel of his body pressed against hers. She ran her hands down Mike's back.

"You feel even better than you look," she said and then propped her head up, letting her eyes travel down his whole body. "I knew you would be fantastic." She grinned, teasingly skimming her hands first down one side of his body and then the other. She could feel his muscles quivering beneath the skin. When her fingers traced a line between his hip bones, Mike moaned huskily.

"Did anyone ever tell you that you have the hands of an artist?" Mike whispered with a throaty laugh, capturing her fingers and bringing them to his lips. Stacy slipped one of her fingers into his mouth, teasing the edge of his tongue with her light touch. Exerting the slightest pressure, she parted his lips and, bending her head down, she slipped her tongue inside, letting her fingers gently caress and stroke his face. Mike's hands massaged Stacy's back, his fingers lovingly moving up and down the exquisite curve that ran from her waist down to her thighs. Stacy's tongue continued flicking and probing the warm, sensual textures of Mike's mouth.

His large hands pressed her more fiercely against him as their kiss grew more intense. Then her mouth sought to taste every inch of his magnificent body. Slowly, provocatively, she ran her tongue down his chest to his navel, drawing tantalizing rings around

113

it in ever-widening circles. Mike's hands clasped her head. Groaning loudly now, he pressed her face against his flesh. Stacy's hand slipped between his slightly parted thighs, duplicating with her fingers the same sensual movements her tongue made on his rock-hard stomach. She brushed tiny kisses across his body, committing every spot to memory.

She thrilled to every inch of him, ecstatic in her discovery that he was even more perfect than she had imagined. She stroked him tenderly, molding him with her hands as though he were her finest creation. She wanted to somehow capture every nuance of his form—to feel, to taste, to know his very essence. As her lips returned to his, she clutched him to her, once more reminding Mike of the hidden strength she possessed.

Gently Mike tugged Stacy's hands from his neck and rolled her over on her back. His eyes, in the morning light, glittered as he gazed at her from head to toe.

"Such an utterly perfect form," he whispered with a smile, his fingers skimming down from her throat to her flat stomach. "More beautiful than any sculpture could ever hope to be."

He bent toward her and placed a feathery kiss on the pulsating center of her throat. Then with his lips he sought every line and curve of her body, his tongue tasting each place his lips joyfully discovered. His soft, moist mouth encircled her tender nipples, tugging, nibbling, kissing them awake. His hands

114

gently cupped each perfectly formed breast. As he moved his lips down the length of her body, languorously running his tongue back and forth over the vulnerable area where her hip and thigh connected, Stacy arched her back, a low, purring sound escaping her throat.

"My beautiful tigress," he murmured as he descended to her thighs, continuing his sensual exploration. Stacy felt passion electrify her body. She writhed in delight as he placed a string of kisses down her inner thigh to her calves. She was beginning to grow frantic with desire, her body crying out to be possessed.

Sensing her mounting need yet wanting to prolong the feelings of each new discovery, he skimmed his mouth down to her toes and playfully nipped them as his fingers stroked the bottoms of her feet. She began to squirm, giggles erupting like little bubbles.

"You're not playing fair," she gasped through her laughter.

He was at the foot of the bed, between her legs. All at once he gripped each ankle and tugged hard, so that she slid down the smooth sheets, ending straddled on top of him.

Her laughter grew deeper and then it disappeared as she felt the intensity of his desire. He buried his head between her breasts as she began to slowly, erotically rake her fingers through his hair, down to his neck and back, caressing the taut muscles as Mike moaned huskily.

Her legs were draped around him, and as he captured an inviting nipple, she clasped her thighs more tightly against his hips. Mike's hands moved down her spine to her bottom. Holding her firmly, he slipped back up the bed with her still locked on his lap. Half-sitting, half-lying, he leaned up against the headboard, holding her in place.

She wrapped her ankles around his back as Mike's fingers reached up to her mass of blond curls. For a second he playfully ruffled her hair, but then his fingers spread out and he brought her head down to his.

Their eyes open, seeking, searching, discovering every nuance of expression, they began to kiss lightly. Mike's tongue traced the lines of Stacy's lips as hers savored the moist softness of his. When Stacy moved past his parted lips to entwine with the velvet smoothness of his tongue, the teasing stopped. Hungrily Mike drew her against him, his mouth passionately taking hers, his tongue darting in and out between her lips in tantalizing, seductively symbolic movements.

As they kissed, their need for each other skyrocketing out of control, Mike grasped her hips, lifting her up slightly for a brief moment, and then thrust himself inside her at last. Then, entwined, Mike guided Stacy onto her back and he began to take her with smooth expert movements, Stacy following his lead, over and beyond the bounds of ecstasy. The release was sublime, and they clung to each other, their damp bodies trembling with pleasure and satisfaction.

Finally they separated. Stacy raised her hands over her head and stretched languorously. As she did, Mike's palm slid down her body, resting on her belly. He could feel the slight tremor beneath the sensitive flesh.

Stacy flung her arm around his waist, nuzzling against him. She pressed her lips to his chest.

"Still fluttering, I see." She laughed softly, placing a kiss on his hardened nipple.

"I doubt the old ticker will ever be the same again. You've wound it up to its maximum capacity, babe."

"Good," she whispered, trailing her index finger down his chest.

Mike brushed the palm of his hand down the length of her back to her buttocks, kissing her all the while with teasingly erotic nibbling bites. He urged her harder against his tight muscular body, his touches arousing her again, just when she had decided she'd never felt this sated in her life. She laughed huskily.

"Are you suggesting seconds already?" She grinned provocatively.

"I thought the first time was just practice. Now comes the real thing," he whispered, pulling her to him.

This time their rhythm was even more in tune. They seemed to require little learning to know what kinds of caresses, what sensitive areas, what pace pleased the other most. It seemed almost as if each had known the other's body intimately for years.

Throughout the morning they made love, rested, made love again. At times they lazily dozed off, but whenever their bodies touched it was as if an electric charge had gone off and once again they would reach out to taste the ecstasy they had discovered.

Finally the two of them rested, their bodies nestled close together. Her speech muffled from exhaustion, Stacy muttered, "Whatever happens, this is one experience I will never forget or ever regret. I'm going to bottle it up and keep it for a lifetime."

He said something in reply, but she was asleep before his words penetrated.

It was almost noon before they woke up again. And then it was only the shrill ring of the phone that made them stir. Sighing contentedly, Stacy stretched out her arm for the phone, still delighting in the feel of Mike's hand resting lightly on her breast.

Joe Turner's gruff, businesslike tone broke her languorous mood. She also felt oddly as if she had just gotten caught with her hand in the cookie jar. She had to smile to herself, thinking of her last conversation with Joe and of how she had been going to make Mike pay. Some payment!

After a cursory greeting, Joe asked for Mike. Shrugging, she rolled over and handed him the phone. Stacy could tell from Mike's slightly stilted tone that he had much the same feeling of being caught cheating as she did. It was ridiculous, but it was nonetheless an odd feeling of guilt they shared. Maybe their having been so adamant about remaining uninvolved was the cause. Or maybe they both knew they had just taken a step that was bound to have some weighty consequences. There was no chance to explore their feelings, as Joe's call was a couched order for Mike to come down to the newsroom and straighten out some cub reporter's mess.

Mike gave Stacy a quick, perfunctory kiss and swiftly threw his clothes on. Stacy could see that he was determined to get out of there in a hurry. She barely had time to say good-bye before he bolted through the front door. She had a feeling his rush was not only due to Joe's request.

Stacy was having her share of mixed emotions as well, including a feeling of panic. "Now what happens," she said softly to herself and then stuck her head under the covers. The side of the bed that Mike had left was still warm. Her moan switched to a warm sigh. She dozed off again.

CHAPTER SEVEN

Stacy had a few brief calls from Mike over the next four days. Each one was the same. He was sorry but he was tied up at the paper. Stacy did not pay attention to the reason. It didn't matter, true or not. She could sense each time she spoke with Mike that he was tense, keyed up. She wasn't doing any better. Finally, he called to tell her he would stop by the following morning. Stacy had been about to insist on getting together. It was high time they talked about what was happening.

When Mike showed up the next day, Stacy was hard at work on a few preliminary small clay models of her male nude. As soon as she opened the door, she realized how much she had missed him. It was a disturbing sensation. Mike came in and strolled over to her worktable, gingerly lifting one of her models.

"It's great."

"That's only a beginning step," she said. Their voices sounded strangely awkward to her.

"Stacy."

"Mike."

They both spoke at the same time.

"You go first," Stacy got in ahead of him.

"I'm leaving in exactly three days, Stacy. You know, for about five minutes after we made love I was actually sure that I could handle this."

"Handle what, Mike?"

He gave her a long, steady look. "Handle fitting you into my life—but it's impossible. I can't change, Stacy. I can't even think about the idea of getting tied down. I've worked for twenty years to get where I am. I'm probably crazy but I love being in the thick of things, risking my neck to get the best damned story any newsman can get. I've always had a kind of cavalier attitude about life. Something like when my number is up, well, at least I'll go down doing what I wanted to be doing. Can you see what I'm talking about? You—us together—it can't work."

"You're telling me? That piece you're holding in your hand that you think is so great—it stinks. As do all the other models and drawings I've tried for the last four days. I can't concentrate. I'll start working and—and there you are. Either I start having X-rated daydreams or else I try to figure out what's

121

going to happen from this point on. I'm already beginning to see my career slipping down the tubes. I keep telling myself I want you to get out of here already so I can work on forgetting you and get back to my real world. Only every time I think about you leaving, I get this terrible pang inside. What a mess. There's no way we could make this thing work. And yet . . ." She let the sentence drift off with a wan smile.

"A regular Romeo and Juliet, huh?"

"Star-crossed lovers, twentieth-century style. The modern woman meets the modern man. Both sacrifice their relationship for their careers. Sounds like it could be a successful play for Broadway." Stacy gave him a half grin even though it hurt.

Mike walked over to her, slipping his arms around her tiny waist. "You are really something, English. I'm never going to forget you."

"That sounds like the closing line of the play," she said, her words a whisper.

"It is. I'll be at the dedication the day after tomorrow, which finishes up my assignment, but I'd rather say good-bye to you without the crowds. Besides, I have some last-minute things to do before I hightail it to London." He looked into Stacy's sad brown eyes, begging her for understanding. They both accepted the hopelessness of their situation and knew it was best not to draw out their suffering.

But to Stacy, the thought of Mike stepping out of her life without any warning was intolerable.

"Just because you're leaving doesn't mean we can't spend the next few days together. I could help you with those last-minute things," she said, a note of pleading in her voice. If he said yes, she reasoned she would at least have a few extra moments with him. They were going to have to last her a lifetime.

"I don't think it makes sense to prolong our agony, Stacy." But she could hear the hedging in his tone. He wasn't finding the thought of saying good-bye any easier than she. "Besides," he continued, "you wouldn't want to—to tag along today. I've got to sit on a hot subway for close to an hour and then spend the afternoon with my mother. Believe me, you would be bored stiff."

"No I wouldn't. I'm crazy about the idea of meeting your mother. I'm positively bursting with curiosity. Anyway, you owe me. I've let you be my shadow for the last two weeks. You only have to give me one day's turn."

"Stacy, honestly, my mom is a terrific lady, but she has a way of going on and on and on. She is going to spend the whole time filling me in on all the comings and goings over the past six months of all five of my brothers and sisters. Then she's going to spend any extra time bemoaning my life, my work, my clothes, and top it off by insisting I get a haircut before I go home. Now, come on, does that sound like an exciting way for you to spend your day?"

"Yep. Let's go."

Mike knew when he was licked. "You are going to

regret this," he said, and to himself he added, "And so am I."

Mike's edginess did not let up. On the long, hot train ride he found himself needing to explain why his mother lived in a rather rundown neighborhood in the Bronx.

"I have been on my mother's back for years now to let me move her into a nicer area. I've offered to buy her a condo in a good neighborhood where I don't have to worry about her getting mugged or God knows what else one of these days."

"Maybe she's proud," Stacy offered. "Doesn't want to feel her son has to support her."

"That may be a small part of it. She claims she loves where she lives. She's been there for thirty years and knows everyone in every apartment on the whole block."

"Well then, if she's happy, that's really what's important, isn't it?"

"Well, I'll tell you the real reason she won't move out of that apartment." He paused, not sure about whether to go on.

Stacy sensed his wariness, as she always did when Mike discussed his private life. She still couldn't understand why he was so reluctant to share anything of his own world with her. His background, his family, his life apart from the paper were still a mystery to her. She knew that she shouldn't push him for more information, but she was consumed with curiosity to learn more about this man who had become so important to her.

She didn't have to ask. Mike smiled wryly and said, "She won't go because she is firmly convinced my dad's spirit is still in the apartment. He died in his sleep twenty-five years ago in their bedroom, and since then she got it into her head that his ghost still resides there. Growing up, we all got used to hearing her talk to Dad if there was a problem or a question. After she discussed it with his—uh—spirit, she would resolve whatever was going on and that would be that. Sound a little loony?"

"No, not really." Stacy smiled gently. "It sounds like your folks must have had a special relationship, and when your father died, your mother probably found his spiritual presence a comfort. I can't see that it could have done any harm."

"What's with you, woman?" He grinned. "I confide one of the deep, dark secrets of my life and you give me brilliant insight and understanding. You keep making it harder and harder for me to leave you." He ruffled her blond curls, sighed and then pretended to concentrate on reading the headlines of a newspaper held by a man across the aisle. Eventually his gaze drifted out the window. They had emerged from the tunnel and were now on an elevated track passing block after block of dilapidated and abandoned apartment buildings. The view saddened Mike. He always felt the Bronx held a dreary kind of colorless, intense heat that inevitably depressed him. He also never failed to feel a rush of anger that his mother wouldn't get out of this deteriorating environment, his father's ghost notwithstanding. Hell, if he was so alive in her mind, why couldn't she just tell his father that she was moving the two of them to a better location? Mike decided he would try this new approach on his mother—not today, though. Today he merely wanted to make it through the visit and get Stacy out of there as fast as possible.

As they walked the two drab blocks to his mother's apartment, Mike kept sneaking glances at Stacy to catch her reaction. This must be quite different from where she grew up, he thought. Pangs of inferiority plagued him as he wondered what she must be thinking of the rundown old buildings and the dirty streets. Stacy's very presence here, with her well-bred style and privileged upbringing, reminded him of his lower-class beginnings. This was yet another reason why they could never make it together, he realized sadly.

Mike looked at Stacy, almost hoping to see some sign of discomfort or look of disdain, but there was none. She looked interested and even a bit intrigued, but that was all. He couldn't even focus his attention on being angry at her, he thought ruefully. She offered him no relief from the gnawing feeling in his gut.

Mike guided her around the children playing on the front stoop. He nodded a cursory hello, trying unsuccessfully to remember their names. Stacy smiled at them, full of friendliness and good cheer. It only added to Mike's escalating bad humor.

As he knocked on the door, he wished he had gotten a chance to call his mother and tell her he was bringing Stacy. He should have made a special point of explaining that she was only someone he was working with. Knowing his mother, he was sure she'd take one look at Stacy and begin ordering wedding invitations.

As soon as his mother, a tiny, robust woman with the same dark features as Mike, opened the door, he knew it was hopeless. He was sure he could see wedding bells in her eyes the moment she saw Stacy. On the way over he had worried about this meeting turning into a fiasco. Now he was confident it was going to be a full-scale disaster.

Mrs. Gallotti swept Stacy into the apartment, chattering away at her and scolding her son for not bringing such a charming young woman to meet her sooner.

"Michael, what is the matter with you? You bring a lovely lady home and you don't even tell your momma first. Look at me, in my housedress. If I had known you were coming I would have cooked my special marinara sauce for you, but now I don't have anything good to give you to eat." Mike had barely gotten the introductions out before his mother's tirade began. "Michael doesn't appreciate it. That's why I don't bother for him alone. He used to make me give him his pasta plain—only a little butter, maybe. He doesn't know what's good." She captured Stacy's arm, ushering her into the living room with Mike following sheepishly behind. Stacy had the distinct impression that Mrs. Gallotti was making note of the thinness of her arm as she held it.

"Well, I adore a good marinara sauce and I rarely get the chance to have it," Stacy said warmly as Mrs. Gallotti hurried over to the sofa, pulling off the plastic cover and practically shoving Stacy down on a cushion.

"It's a promise. Next time, give me some notice and I'll make you a sauce you'll never forget. My husband, Anthony, god rest his soul"—she clearly looked over her shoulder as if she was including her husband in the conversation—"used to say, 'Momma, this is a tomato sauce fit for the pope.' " She sat down beside Stacy, her arms barely folding over her generous stomach.

"So tell me, how did my son find such a beauty? I can't count the number of years since he's brought a girl home for me to meet. You remember that big lanky one you brought to dinner that time, Michael?" she said and looked over at her son, who was sitting across from her in a club chair that was still ensconced in plastic film. He looked painfully uncomfortable. He barely remembered the girl his mother was talking about. She was someone he'd met on the paper while he was still a cub reporter. If he remembered correctly, he never saw her afterward. The thing he had not forgotten was that he had vowed never to bring another date home to Momma until after the wedding, should that ever happen. How had he let Stacy talk him into breaking still another vow?

He sat back in the chair, the plastic cover crinkling and sticking to him. It was the least of his concerns. He tried to think of some excuse to get the two of them out of here in a hurry. Meanwhile Stacy and his mother busily chatted away, Stacy telling her how they had met, thankfully skipping many of the details.

Stacy was enchanted by Mike's mother. She was the warmest, most effusive woman she had ever met. Stacy felt immediately accepted and completely at home. There was no doubt that Mrs. Gallotti's apartment had seen better days. The paint was beginning to chip on the ceilings; the wood floors had a worn, well-used look. Even the ornate upholstered furniture, ever guarded against dust and dirt by the heavy plastic slipcovers, had faded with time. But the house was meticulously clean. More important, Stacy felt that this house held love. Cherished pictures of family, children and grandchildren decorated almost every tabletop, every wall. Little objects, like handmade ashtrays and lopsided boxes, that Stacy supposed had been made by some of the grandchildren, were proudly displayed on the coffee table.

Mrs. Gallotti spent most of her time talking with Stacy, turning to Mike occasionally for affirmation or information, both of which Mike gave reluctantly.

Occasionally she would criticize something about him, like his bad temper or the casual way he dressed. She even badgered him a bit about his hair, just as Mike had told Stacy she would. It was the only time he managed a warm grin. What struck Stacy most was that with all Mike's grumblings and his mother's tender nagging, there seemed a tight, loving bond between them. It showed in Mike's eyes despite his discomfort, and it positively glowed from every pore of Mrs. Gallotti. This boy, her youngest, was her treasured pride and joy. Everything she said about this son was accompanied by a burst of love and satisfaction. Mike was special. That was something Stacy knew as well.

Mike tried to put his foot down when his mother started for the bureau to retrieve old pictures of him as a young boy, but Stacy was dying to see them and voiced her desire. Mrs. Gallotti merely waved her hand in the air in the direction of her son and went off happily to the other room for the pictures.

When she stepped out of the living room, Mike muttered, "You're really enjoying this, aren't you?"

"I am. Your mother is an absolute delight. I can't imagine how you could have thought I'd be bored," Stacy said truthfully, but she could see that Mike didn't believe her. He was wearing his disgruntled feelings on his sleeve, thinking that what Stacy was really enjoying was seeing him suffer. Mike didn't say another word.

Mrs. Gallotti came in laden with photograph albums. Stacy hurried to help her.

"Momma, what are you doing? We have to get going in a few minutes. It'll take a year to go through those pictures," Mike said irritably.

"Always in a hurry, that son of mine. Always in hurry. Dash here, dash there . . . hurry, hurry, hurry. How many times have I told you—relax a little, stay put." To Stacy she added, "I give up. Maybe you'll have a better chance. Something to stay home for, huh, Michael?"

Mrs. Gallotti and Stacy again settled comfortably on the couch, this time sitting closer together as Mike's mother began explaining the photos.

"You were an adorable kid, Michael," Stacy said and smiled at him.

"Yeah, a regular doll!" Mike muttered. "Could you skip over a few, Mom? Really, we—we've got an appointment in—in an hour."

Stacy gave him a questioning grimace, knowing full well he was lying through his teeth. But then she gave him a warm smile and came to his defense. "Mike is right, Mrs. Gallotti. But I do want to see a few more pictures of Michael before we go off."

Mike smiled his appreciation at Stacy, and then a wave of depression swept over him. The reality of their parting hit him straight between the eyes, the pain of it blinding him for a second. Mrs. Gallotti caught the change in her son's expression.

"What is it, Michael? You sick?" Her voice was filled with immediate concern.

"No, Ma. I'm fine. I was just thinking about something." He flashed a quick glance at Stacy. The look in her eyes told him she had guessed his thoughts. She looked back down at the album, a sharp desire to cry almost overwhelming her. This felt like a beginning to Stacy. But it was an end, she realized sadly.

Mrs. Gallotti's steady stream of talk about Mike helped Stacy get herself together.

"So stubborn. Would he ever tell me if he was sick? No, never. That time when you were in the Philippines"—she waved an accusing finger at her son—"did you even let me know you'd been beaten up? Laying in a hospital in some godforsaken place, and I don't know a thing about it." She turned to Stacy. "Comes home with bandages everywhere. Then he tells me."

"Come on, Ma. I had a couple of Band-Aids over my eye. It was nothing."

His mother paid no attention, continuing as she took Stacy's hand. "I wish you luck. Me, I've been at my wit's end with this child of mine since he was old enough to talk. Always stubborn. One time—one time when he was maybe eight years old, I reached my limit. I hate to admit—"

Mike leaped up. "Not that story again, Momma. Now, enough is enough. Stacy doesn't want to hear every ridiculous detail about me from age one on

132

up." He strode to the couch and took Stacy's other hand, trying to pull her up. Stacy didn't cooperate.

"Hold it, Michael," she said with a grin. "Your mom was just getting to the best part. And I'm not leaving until I hear the story. Even if it means being late for our meeting," she added pointedly.

Mike threw up his hands in total disgust. "Well, if you ladies don't mind, I've heard this story before. I'm going to the kitchen for a beer. I assume you remembered to buy some," he grumbled, not waiting for a response.

Mrs. Gallotti watched her son go. "Besides being stubborn, he's also sensitive." She chuckled. Shouting so Mike would hear, she said, "Stacy should know what she's getting into."

Mike peered out the kitchen door. "I hate to disappoint you, Ma, but Miss English is not about to get into anything. I suppose it's useless to try to make you see that she didn't come along today to meet her future mother-in-law."

"Who said anything about mother-in-law? You said she's a friend—so she's a friend. Sometimes friendships are the best foundation for something more . . . who knows what the future holds in store for any of us?"

"You're hopeless, Ma." He had to grin. "But you'd better be careful. If you're so crazy about my friend, then you shouldn't be telling her about all my lousy traits."

"Forewarned is forearmed." She grinned back at

her son. "So anyway, Stacy, where was I? Oh, yes. This one day Michael comes home from school and informs me he's got to have a three-speed bicycle. So I ask how much is this three-speed bike. When he tells me, I tell him the bike his cousin Tomás gave him had plenty enough speed. So he decides to go on a hunger strike. Two days that boy wouldn't eat a thing. His father, may he rest in peace"—again she looked over her shoulder rather than up toward the sky—"was about to take his belt to the boy. Never before did Michael get him so angry. But I said to be patient. He'll get hungry, he'll eat. But no. Suppertime comes the next night—I make my best linguine with my finest tomato sauce—he won't touch it. I sit next to him, I plead with him, I yell at him. He sat there with his arms crossed, his mouth zippered closed. So finally . . . I got so mad, so frustrated. I wasn't even thinking, I was so angry. I just lifted up the bowl of spaghetti and—and—" His mother displayed an impish grin. "I turned the whole bowl of spaghetti over his head."

Stacy burst into laughter. The image of Mike sitting at the dining table with spaghetti on his head and tomato sauce dripping down his face had to be the funniest thing she'd ever imagined. Mike's mother joined in the laughter, first assuring Stacy the spaghetti had been only lukewarm when she dumped it on him.

"I'll tell you," she said with a chuckle, "he never asked for that three-speed bike again." Pausing for a moment, she added, "Of course, since then he's refused to eat my tomato sauce."

Stacy laughed again. "He probably figured he was safer without the sauce. It has to be a lot less messy to get dry spaghetti dumped on your head."

Mrs. Gallotti laughed heartily, tears shining in her eyes. When Mike walked in he found his mother's arm around Stacy, the two of them happily howling.

"If you have both had enough laughs on me for one afternoon, can we call it a day?" Mike had to smile to himself. He never had forgotten that spaghetti episode, and eventually had even found it funny. However, it made him uncomfortable to see Stacy having a laugh at his expense. Again he imagined the contrast between sedate family dinners when she was growing up, and what his own had been like.

Before they left, his mother made him promise to get a haircut before he went to London and also promise to bring Stacy back for another visit. He knew he would not keep either of those promises, but he muttered an agreement about both.

Outside Mike started looking for a taxi to take them back to Manhattan. After several minutes of searching without any success, Stacy suggested they return by subway.

"I may not be in your league, English," he snapped at her. "But believe it or not, I do earn enough money to spring for a cab on occasion."

"Who said anything about how much money

you've got?" she retorted, "It just seems like a waste . . ."

Just then a cab finally came along. Mike hailed it, and when it pulled over to the curb, he opened the door and patiently waited for her to get in. Shrugging and muttering under her breath, Stacy stepped in.

For the first twenty minutes or so neither of them spoke. Actually Stacy made a few attempts, but Mike's sullen expression caused her to change her mind each time.

Finally she couldn't stand it anymore.

"What is it, Gallotti? Can't stand that I broke through your precious privacy? Does it really make you that mad that I learned a little bit about the real Mike Gallotti?"

"I don't appreciate people laughing at my expense; especially people sitting up in their ivory towers casting deprecating, smug smiles in my direction. You got a taste of how the other half lives and you had your fun with it. Let me tell you something, lady—"

"No, let me tell *you* something, mister," she cut in icily. "Your mother happens to be one of the nicest, most loving women I have ever had the good fortune to meet. Do you have any idea how lucky you are, Michael Gallotti, to have a mother like that? A mother who worships the ground you walk on, whose every word about you is filled with joy, admiration, love. Every one of those photos of you and your whole family positively glowed with happiness and affection. Do you have any idea how utterly

136

jealous I feel? The only pictures my family has of me were all taken at graduations and society events by professional photographers, and they wouldn't fill up half an album. The only thing any one of my photos reflects is the cool, well-bred, untouched life I led. So don't start giving me speeches about my being some snob looking down on this scene. If anyone is the snob around here, it's you." She poked her finger into his chest several times for emphasis.

Mike broke out into a smile. "I said before, English, you have a way with words. You know just how to put a dumb, loud-mouth guy right in his place." When he spotted the tears in her eyes, he reached out and hugged her to him with a deep sigh. "Do you think Romeo and Juliet suffered as much as we do?" he whispered tenderly and smiled.

Stacy slipped an arm around his waist and said nothing. Tears rolled down her cheeks.

"I could use a drink. I think you could probably use one too," he said, gently stroking her back.

She lifted her head and looked directly up at him. "It isn't a drink I need, Mike."

He bent down and kissed her lips. It wasn't a drink he needed, either. Holding each other in a staunch embrace against the winds of reality, they rode back to Stacy's loft.

CHAPTER EIGHT

As the cab pulled up in front of Stacy's building, she thought for a moment about the fact that she had never once been to Mike's apartment. Except for this visit to his mother, she had never really entered his world. She found herself wanting to know so much more about him. She wanted to see him at his work, where he lived; to know more about how he spent his time, what music he liked, whether he enjoyed football or baseball. Then suddenly she realized none of that mattered anymore. He would soon be flying out of her life forever.

Stacy hadn't even begun to make sense of her feelings for Mike. There simply hadn't been enough time. Her thoughts reached back to when she had been in Paris so long ago, the only other time she had ever thought she was in love. Only much later, after the pain of that ending had abated, could she admit that what she had felt was really infatuation. Was it any different now?

Telling herself she knew better now didn't help as much as it should have. Maybe she wasn't already head over heels in love with Michael Gallotti, but she was feeling dangerously off balance. It wouldn't be very hard to tip over completely, given time. But, she reminded herself, there was no time. The thought caused her more pain than she was willing to admit.

As they rode up in the elevator, Stacy wound her arms around Mike's neck and pulled his head down toward hers. She kissed him gently at first but then with such growing passion that when their lips at last separated, Mike grinned. "Hold on, honey. I know how much you go for unusual settings for making love, but an elevator floor?"

Stacy tried to smile up at him, but she couldn't shake the sense of finality that was enveloping her. This was the last time she and Mike would make love, the last time she would feel his warmth and strength, the last time they would share the intimacy that bound them body and soul. How was she ever going to live without him? And then the nagging realization: how could she ever live with him—or he with her? They had been over all that ground, and there was no point in rehashing it.

When they stepped into her apartment, Mike swung her around and took her in his arms. He could feel her trembling against him. When he looked down at her, there were tears in the corners of her eyes. He didn't feel that far from tears himself. He, too, was painfully aware that this would be their last time together. It had to be. Once he left, he knew he had to stay away. No popping in to see her when he was in town, no casual get-togethers. He couldn't handle it, and he doubted she could, either. Everything comes to an end, he told himself philosophically, but somehow he couldn't bring himself to believe it.

"Stacy," he said with a tender smile, "don't you start crying now or the two of us are going to flood this apartment."

"Oh, Mike," she said and sniffed loudly. "I don't want to sob through our last time together. I want it to be filled with happiness. I want to take hold of this moment and pretend no other exists."

"No other moment does exist," he whispered, placing his hands lightly on her shoulders.

She gazed up at him, her expression filled with love, and she smiled.

Without a word he began undressing her. Sensually, deliberately, he slid his hands from her shoulders, palms skimming over her breasts to her waist. Gently he tugged her white eyelet blouse out of the waistband of her slacks. Beginning at the bottom, he undid each button. When they were all open, he slid his hands inside the blouse, his fingers trailing up her midriff and catching hold of the clasp at the front of her bra. Deftly he unfastened it.

Then, as though he were unveiling the most exquisite sculpture, he tenderly slid the blouse off her shoulders, letting it fall in a feathery motion to the floor. He had never seen a more sensual sight as this small, perfectly voluptuous beauty in her pink slacks and half-undone lacy white bra standing before him. He reached out and untied the drawstring of her pants. They loosened enough for them to fall provocatively below her narrow waist.

"God, you're beautiful," he murmured, his breathing shallow and uneven. Part of him wanted to take her on the spot, impatient to have her fully. But he did not want to hurry this last experience. He longed to stretch out this moment as long as possible. He desperately wanted time to stand still.

Stacy gazed up at him, basking in Mike's reverence. She gently shook her shoulders, letting her bra slip to the floor. Mike tugged at the waistband of her slacks, and now they, too, easily fell. Stacy stepped out of them, clad only in a pair of lacy bikini panties.

Stacy unbuttoned Mike's shirt, her glittering brown eyes warming him with pleasure. Her fingers spread out across his chest. "That first day when you walked in here and I ordered you to get undressed" —she grinned impishly—"I was not seeing only form and lines."

"You weren't?" he asked, arching his brow. Stacy

removed his shirt, her hands freer to meander over his tanned, warm flesh.

"Not that I didn't appreciate your body as an artist, mind you." She threaded her way down to his tan chinos and leisurely opened his leather belt. "But I have to admit my attraction was a might more personal."

"Not very professional of you, English," he admonished with a teasing grin. His smile faded as she eased her fingers beneath his waistband to undo the button of his trousers.

Within moments they were both fully unclothed. Their need for each other overtook any desire to stretch time. They barely made it to the sofa. Mike's strong arms around her waist arched her to him, his touch obliterating all other sensations. He pressed her neck with a firm pressure, drawing Stacy's lips to his, her mouth opening as they met. Stacy kissed him with fiery urgency, her need for him erupting in tingling bursts of desire all through her body. Pinned to him, she was his willing prisoner, taking abandoned pleasure out of the way his hands shifted from her back up to her shoulders and then tantalizingly slid down to her buttocks. Then both hands caught hold of her waist, and he slid her up easily so that now he had access to those full, lush breasts, the rosy nipples already hardening. When Mike skimmed his tongue along one nipple, then the other, they grew pulsatingly erect. He captured one sweet bud in his mouth, his lips tugging gently as his tongue circled her nipple. Stacy arched her back, her hands pressing down on his broad shoulders, allowing Mike greater movement. Mike's hand cupped her other breast, his mouth still treasuring the taste of her.

He sensed her mounting urgency. For a moment he buried his head in the silken valley between her breasts, and then with a swift motion he pulled her down, his mouth spreading over her lips as he moved inside Stacy with an urgency that matched hers. His fingers encompassed her narrow hips, helping her to move in response to his ever-increasing thrusts. When Stacy cried out with a wild, fiery abandon, Mike yielded to his own release. She sighed deeply as she fell back on top of him, filled with soaring contentment.

Mike gently stroked her face, moving the blond wisps of hair away from her cheek and forehead. He placed a warm kiss on her temple. When she lifted her head slightly to look at him, her eyes met his loving gaze.

"Stacy, I—"

"No, Mike," she cut him off, pressing her fingers to his lips. "Don't say anything that's going to get me all teary-eyed again. There will be plenty of that after you go." She smiled bravely.

He cupped her face in his hands. "My beautiful, courageous lover." He punctuated each word with a kiss. "Will I be on safe ground if I tell you I'm hungry?" He gave her a love pat on her bottom. Stacy rolled off him, landing in a kneeling position on the rug. She ran her fingertips across his chest, then bent and placed a moist kiss on his firm, hard stomach.

"Uhmm. On second thought I'm not that hungry," he murmured, turning his head to her. "I like you on your knees for a change." He grinned seductively.

Stacy placed a warm, tantalizing kiss on his aroused flesh and then gave him a provocative grin. "Oh, you do, do you? So you like your women subservient!" As she spoke her hands stroked his body with an intimate knowledge that evoked a deep moan of pleasure from Mike. Then he slid down on the rug beside her. His growing hunger had little to do with food.

Later, as Mike sat watching Stacy search through the refrigerator for some dinner, he felt warm and contented. Never had he experienced lovemaking so fulfilling and exquisite. Stacy peered over her shoulder.

"You sure you don't want quiche? I still have another one in the freezer."

"Let's not stretch our luck. Stick to something unburnable."

She pulled out some cold chicken and leftover salad. "This will have to do. You do eat chicken legs, don't you?"

"I love all kinds of legs," he teased, catching her leg beneath her light cotton robe. He bent, placing a warm, wet kiss on the back of her thigh. "Mmmm. Delicious. How about if I serve you up for dinner tonight?"

"Control your cannibalistic tendencies, Gallotti. That was something your mother never warned me about."

"Mothers don't know everything," he teased as she wriggled out of his grasp.

They continued to banter lightly, both successfully pretending there would be no tomorrow.

And then, over coffee, Stacy asked abruptly, "What is your assignment in London? That city is not ripe with danger now."

"Not every assignment I go out on is filled with peril, Stacy. This one is to cover the upcoming parliamentary elections." Her question and his response brought them both back to reality. Mike wasn't happy about it.

Stacy wasn't either, but she couldn't stop. "How did you get beaten up in the Philippines?"

He gave her a puzzled look.

"You know. The time you came back home all bandaged."

"You're as bad as my mother, English. Two little Band-Aids do not 'all bandaged up' make."

"How did it happen?" she persisted, ignoring his teasing smile.

"What's the point of—"

"I just want to know, Mike."

"Okay. My photographer and I were covering a

145

story in some outback village when a group of insurgents showed up. Tom snapped some pictures. The leader saw us, grabbed Tom's camera and smashed it. Tom took a poke at the guy's solar plexis, and the next thing the two of us were in an all-out brawl with the whole pack of them. Some soldiers happened along, they joined in, and everyone had a grand go at each other."

"You make it sound like fun and games." The irritation in her tone was unmistakable.

Mike slid his chair back from the table. Patting his knee, he said, "Come here and sit down. I want to tell you something."

Stacy hesitated for a moment and then went and sat on on his lap. He put his arm around her waist.

"Stacy, it's no use your worrying about me. It won't do you any good, any more than it makes sense for me to start worrying about you falling off a ladder one day when you're working on one of your massive sculptures. Or," he said more softly, "worrying about whether some society guy or sexy male model is going to come along and . . ." He didn't finish the sentence.

"Nothing like this is ever going to happen to me again, Mike. If only things were different; if only *we* were different. I know your leaving is for the best—for both of us. But damnit—" She broke off, resting her cheek against his. "It hurts like hell."

"I know, baby, I know." He caressed her neck, letting his tears fall. "I'm hurting, too. And there will

146

never be anything like this again for me, either." He took her by the shoulders and eased her back enough for her to look at him. "Do you believe me?"

She merely nodded. She did believe that what had happened between the two of them was something that occurred once in a lifetime. She trailed her fingers through his ruffled hair.

"How about dessert?" she whispered.

He slipped one arm under her legs and lifted her in his arms. When he set her down on the bed, the summer sun was just beginning to fade. For a long time he held her close to him, reveling in the feel of her warm body, which seemed to fit so perfectly against his. Then they began to make love slowly, languidly, with an intimacy and assurance that belied the short time they had known each other. Mike gazed into Stacy's eyes. They were filled with radiant anticipation, her creamy skin aglow with passion.

This time their lovemaking was tender beyond compare; every touch, every kiss filled with sweet surrender. They moved together as though they were floating. They felt suspended in time and space, intent only on the pleasure they gave and the love they received.

Afterward Stacy looked up at the sky, surprised to see the start of sunset. She hadn't even noticed the growing dusk, but now a soft blue haze poked through the clouds.

Mike stretched. "I'd better get going, Stacy." His voice was sad.

She shifted slightly to face him. "Don't leave, Mike. Just this once I want to wake up in the morning with you by my side. Please, Mike. There's going to be all the rest of our lives to be apart. Let's not give time any more of us than we have to."

Her words and the touch of her hand tore into the very fiber of his being. Fiercely, savagely he grabbed her to him. He held onto her for dear life. Finding her lips, he plundered them with hot, searing kisses. He wanted her; he wanted to possess her. He never wanted to let her go. His fiery passion provoked Stacy's own explosive need. They assaulted each other with burning desire. They wanted to consume each other, trying to erase the biting ache festering inside them. Lust and yearning fired them, consumed them, carried them to a peak of ecstasy so powerful they collapsed afterward, not even having the energy to hold one another.

It took some time for them to catch their breath. Stacy stared up at the sky. It was streaked with a brilliant purple and then softer, muted tones of red and yellow. It was rare to see such a burst of color in a New York City sunset. But then this had been a rare day.

"Mike," Stacy whispered, her eyes fixed on the sky. "Let's make a pact."

"What kind of pact?" He eased his arm under her shoulders.

"When we're both old and gray—when you're too decrepit to go gallivanting around the world on dangerous assignments and I'm too weak to lift my chisel —let's meet again."

He gazed up at the rainbow sky, holding her against him in a cherished embrace. "That's a deal, English. But you'll have to marry me then. I don't intend to spend my last days living in sin. What would my mother say?" He laughed softly.

"We'll get ourselves a couple of matched rocking chairs, sit out on a porch somewhere, creaking away and watching all our remaining sunsets together," she murmured, her voice dreamy.

"Add a couple of mint juleps to that scene and it's perfect."

"Mint juleps—I promise."

They fell asleep in each other's arms. Stacy dreamed of southern skies, tall glasses of minty elixir —and Mike.

In the morning, just as she had wished, Mike lay beside her. He was already awake, his eyes warmly caressing her as she opened her sleepy eyes and stretched. Only a whispered good morning and she was in his arms. Their bodies pressed together, desire swept over them like a windstorm. They clung to each other, hungry to taste all the pleasure they had experienced the night before, and more—new touches, new embraces, ever searching to give all they had, to receive all there was to get. They wanted to experience enough of each other to last a lifetime,

Stacy thought afterward as she lay cradled in Mike's loving arms. This had to last a lifetime.

The spell was broken once they had to face the start of a new day—the day before Mike left. He was edgy. She was unusually quiet. Finally he told her he had to go to the paper to finish his profile of her.

"Shall I bring you a copy tonight?" Mike asked. "Joe made it clear I had to get your okay before it went to press."

Stacy shook her head. She trusted Mike implicitly, and the idea of reading his article depressed her. It was a symbol; it had brought them together, and finishing it signified the end.

"No," she said out loud. "I'll read it in the *Globe* —after you've gone. Just omit some of my less appealing qualities," she said with a smile.

"You have none, English. None at all." He stepped toward her.

Stacy held up her hand, halting him. "Mike, let's say good-bye now. I thought I could hold up till the end, but—but we've had our time. We've had it to ourselves. Each of us has a lot to do—before tomorrow. It can't be the same. Just go, okay? No drawn-out good-byes; no see you around's. I'm going to give myself a couple of hours to cry my heart out, then I'm going to try my damn best to pull myself together and get on with my life."

Mike nodded his agreement. He wanted to tell her something—something that would ease the pain. But there was nothing to say that could help either of them. It was better simply to leave. He made a poor attempt to smile, took one last look around the loft, one last aching look at Stacy and walked to the door.

Before he stepped outside he turned for a moment. "I'll never forget you, Stacy." Stacy mouthed the echo of his words. He left, closing the door softly behind himself.

Stacy did as she had said. She cried her heart out. She was, however, not very successful at glueing the pieces back together. Some of them seemed too far gone.

CHAPTER NINE

The dedication, sedate and restrained as Stacy had requested, was going off without a hitch. Stacy was standing near the mayor. Derek Morgan, his lips pursed in disapproval, stood off to the side. He was still convinced that jugglers would have been the perfect addition to the ceremony.

Mike was in the front of the crowd, next to Sam and Annie. Stacy's eyes kept veering toward him no matter how emphatically she told herself not to focus on him. She would be asked to speak as soon as the mayor's speech drew to a close. He was still going strong. Stacy thought if he reiterated how peace and harmony were to be the city's guiding words one more time, she was going to scream. He did. She didn't.

Her speech of thanks was brief. It reflected her pride in her work and her pleasure that this sculpture had been chosen to grace the new center. She kept her eyes directed away from Mike, focused somewhere on the back of the crowd. The mayor shook her hand. The other city officials on the podium followed suit. When it was over, she looked in Mike's direction. He was gone.

In the weeks that followed Mike's departure, Stacy did her best to put all thoughts of him out of her mind. Whenever she passed a newsstand, she forced herself not to look. It was a poor shot at denial, but she didn't want to see Mike's bylines; she didn't want to know what dangerous situation he happened to be in the midst of at any particular time. All through the summer she was fairly successful.

She did, however, read his profile of her and the review he wrote of her *Peace and Harmony* sculpture. His articles were glowing tributes to her as a person and an artist. But they were more than that. Between the lines Stacy could read the depth of Mike's admiration and his understanding of who she really was. Mike Gallotti had uncovered the true Stacy English, just as he had promised, and he had left her exposed and defenseless. But not once did she wish she hadn't met him. She had thought time would help her forget him, but as the days since his departure lengthened into weeks, she realized the pain only became stronger. Stacy was certain now that she had fallen in love with Mike, and for all the anguish his absence caused, he had given her something priceless that she would cherish the rest of her life. Many times she found herself wondering if they could have made a go of it—somehow blended their careers and their relationship into a successful whole. But whenever she thought it possible, she reminded herself that both she and Mike were too independent. Each led a life that left no room for the other.

She had almost made it successfully past the newsstand one morning when a stout, elderly man blocked her path. Picking up a copy of the *Globe,* he grumbled loudly about all the craziness going on today in El Salvador. "Another Vietnam," he snarled. "You mark my words," he said, turning abruptly to Stacy, forcing her to a stop, "this is the start of the nuclear holocaust." He held the paper in front of her, tapping his finger angrily at the El Salvador article, the lead story on the front page.

Of course, it was Mike's article. His name bounced off the page at her as though it had been written in 3D.

Stacy couldn't concentrate on her work for the rest of the day. Zeke Stewart had been modeling for her since Mike had gone. Her work had been going pretty well, everything considered, but today was hopeless, and she gave Zeke the afternoon off. He was thrilled to have the extra time to study for his law boards.

After Zeke left, Stacy returned to the same newsstand and bought the *Globe*. Standing there, she read the article. The old man had been right. This tiny Central American country had become a hotbed of violence and madness. And Mike was right in the thick of it. Walking back to her loft, she felt a mounting terror. Mike's words played over and over in her mind. "There's no point in worrying about me." Terrific advice, she growled out loud, slamming her door closed as she stepped into her loft.

By evening she had calmed down. Mike had been in hundreds of dangerous spots. Maybe he was like a cat and had nine lives. The only problem was she had no idea how many he had already used up. That night her dreams were filled with exploding bombs, army tanks and soldiers. And leading all the attacks, naturally, was Mike.

It was a relief to wake up the next morning.

By the time Zeke arrived, she was feeling better. She was also filled with excited anticipation, because this was to be the day she would begin the actual sculpture. She had made hundreds of sketches, dozens of working models, and today she would work on the massive stone itself.

She became so engrossed in her work, she didn't hear the phone at first. Zeke had to tell her it was ringing.

Stacy hated interruptions when she was at work. Usually she took the receiver off the hook, but she had forgotten to do that today.

She recognized Joe Turner's voice immediately. She also sensed that something was wrong, even though it took him a minute or two to get to the point.

"Stacy, I'm going to tell you this because, like I told you before, I know you and Mike very well. He never said a word to me, mind you, but some things don't have to be spelled out."

"Joe," Stacy snapped, irritated by his long-winded approach. "What's wrong?" Her heart was beating a mile a minute. "Something's happened to him." It was more a statement than a question.

"Well, like I figured, the two of you really clicked. I thought you might. Probably I shouldn't have got this whole thing started. Not that I chose Mike to do the story for that reason. Hell no. But I'm not surprised—"

"Joe!"

"He's okay, Stacy. Take it easy."

"Damnit, Joe Turner, for an old newshound you sure as hell use up a lot of words."

He chuckled, but then his voice grew serious. "Now before you erupt, let me have my say. Mike's up at Roosevelt Hospital—"

"The hospital!"

"I told you to let me finish. The damn fool stepped right into the fray down in El Salvador and went off trying to find the rebel commander for an exclusive interview. I gave him a direct order to stay out of that zone, but would he listen? So he got himself shot

156

instead." Quickly, before Stacy had time to react, he added, "It's little more than a flesh wound in his arm." The bullet, he knew, had penetrated deeper than the flesh and Mike was going to be laid up for a few weeks anyway, but Joe saw no reason to upset Stacy any more than necessary. He got to the real point of his call.

"The thing is, Stacy, Mike is determined to go back and track down that interview. Let's face it, I can order him till kingdom come to stay away from the rebel zone. But the only way I could get him to obey is to fire him. And I hate even to think about that. What I thought was—well, maybe you could have some influence over him. You know, go over and visit him at the hospital, talk to him . . ."

First Mrs. Gallotti, and now Joe Turner had this fantasy that she had some kind of magical power over Mike. Nothing could be further from the truth, Stacy thought. She couldn't imagine for a moment that Mike would take orders from her.

Still, she had to see him. She had known that as soon as Joe had told her Mike was in the hospital. They had promised to keep away from each other, but she was not going to keep her word now. She loved him and had to know he was really all right. She promised herself she'd leave then, stuffing her pain into her back pocket. Mike wouldn't have to know anything except that she cared enough to check on him.

How Mike was going to feel about her showing up

was another story. She remembered how adamant he had been about keeping their distance. Stacy was certain Mike was not going to be too happy to see her, but she didn't care. Anyway, she comforted herself, they both usually did what they wanted to do. She was merely being true to form. The thought that she was more than a little tense about seeing Mike again got successfully camouflaged—for the moment, anyway.

Suddenly remembering Zeke, who stood quietly by, looking concerned, she briefly explained that a good friend was in the hospital and she had to go see him. Zeke nodded understandingly and offered to give her a lift on his motorcycle. Stacy, quickly unbuttoning her smock, jumped at his offer. She did not want to waste any time.

A few minutes later, walking into the sterile entrance of the hospital, she remembered Joe's comment that Mike's injury was only a flesh wound. She knew he had lied. No flesh wound kept someone laid up in the hospital for weeks. But she hadn't bothered to pursue it with Joe. She would find out herself.

When she stepped out of the elevator on the fourth floor, she spotted Mrs. Gallotti coming out of one of the rooms. She looked older and tired, but when she saw Stacy her face brightened. Mrs. Gallotti took her hand, patting it gently.

"He's fine, Stacy. Take that long look off your face. We just spent the last ten minutes shouting at each other. That's a good sign, right?" She squeezed

Stacy's hand. "Pay no attention if he growls at you too. He insists he can go home today and he's boiling because the doctor says he has to stay three, maybe four days. I told him to come home with me when he leaves the hospital. But he's so stubborn—well, you know that. He can manage fine, he says. How's he going to manage fine with his arm all bandaged up and in a sling?" She saw how anxious Stacy was to be with him. "Go, Stacy. Go to him. Maybe he'll listen to you."

Stacy merely sighed, patted Mrs. Gallotti on the shoulder and walked to the door of Mike's room. She hesitated for a moment before opening it. It hit her how scared she was. Not because of Mike's injury; Joe may have lied, but Mike's mother had eased her mind on that account. No, it was seeing him again that was making her stomach do somersaults and her pulse race like mad. What would it be like to see him after all this time?

It was like coming home.

As she stepped into the room, their eyes met instantly, and all fear left her. His hair was a little longer, his eyes reflected strain and exhaustion, and his arm was in a sling, as Mrs. Gallotti had warned. Otherwise he was the same. She remembered the first moment she'd set eyes on him and the feelings he had stirred in her then. This time she made no attempt at restraint—at least, inwardly. On the surface she remained cool. After all, they had agreed not to meet

159

again. Mike, she could see, was already looking wary.

"Hi, Mike." She smiled and walked closer.

"Who squealed—my mother?"

"Joe."

"I told him not to call you." He knitted his thick brows together, looking fierce.

"I guess he doesn't take orders any better than you do."

"So that's it. He sent you along to talk some sense into me. Well, save your breath, English. As soon as they let me out of this jail I'm heading straight back to El Salvador."

"Straight back into the line of another bullet?" she asked bitingly.

"Hazards of the trade," he quipped. "All in a day's work. And I've got a few more days to put in before I finish getting what I want."

"Do you always have to get everything you want?" she snapped, her anger and frustration steadily escalating.

"Not everything, Stacy. There are some things in life I can't have."

His words produced a moment of quiet in the midst of the storm. Their eyes met in intimate understanding. But then Mike swiftly collected himself.

"Nothing has changed, Stacy. We both know that."

"Mike, forget everything else for a minute." She

sat down on the bed beside him. "Can't you let this story go? Joe doesn't want you to go after it."

"Stacy, don't be naive. Sure, Joe doesn't want me to get my head blown off in the process of getting that interview, but if I come home with it in a neat little package, he's going to slap me on the back, hand me my next raise and send me right back out again."

"Then why did he tell me if you didn't stay off this one he was seriously thinking about firing you?" She stretched the truth a little, for a good cause.

Mike smiled broadly. "Do you know how many times Joe has threatened to fire me? Probably right before he handed me every promotion and every raise. He isn't running a social service agency, Stacy." Then, more pointedly, he added, "And I don't appreciate people dropping in on missions of mercy. That's one of the reasons I stay unattached." Mike felt as if Stacy were interfering in things that were none of her business. He had meant it when he'd told her he always did what he wanted and went where he chose. No one was going to start telling him what was best for him. He could feel his muscles constrict, sense himself readying for the fight. And yet, deeper down, he felt Stacy's caring and warmth, understood her fears—even wanted to allay them somehow. But he couldn't. It would mean giving something more—giving a part of himself he had never given to anyone.

Seeing her again convinced him of something he'd been fighting since that day they'd said good-bye. He loved her. Simple as that. Only it wasn't simple at all. There was no chance he was going to let Stacy into his world. He had no intention of getting himself shackled.

Shackled! That word kept running through his head. His dad had stayed shackled to his wife, his kids, his home. He'd had a dream—Mike's mother had always laughed at it and said his father was crazy—but his pop had had a fine tenor voice and had wanted to sing professionally. Gina Gallotti put her foot down before he had the chance to test his dream. He had responsibilities, obligations—only gypsies did the kinds of things he wanted to do. So his dad stayed home, became a brick mason, worked his fingers to the bone—and died before he reached his forty-fifth birthday. So what did his mother get in the end? A spirit instead of flesh and blood for a husband. And what did his father get from all those years of sacrificing his dreams? Nothing, as far as Mike could see.

Well, there was no way he was going to end up like that.

His face rigid, his hazel eyes dark with anger, he said, "I've gotten along just fine for the past twenty years on this paper doing things my way. I don't think I need anyone at this stage of the game to play nursemaid."

Stacy glared at him without saying a word. Then she slid down off the bed, walked to the door and opened it. Glancing back over her shoulder, she said, "Good luck Gallotti. You're going to need it if you plan to make that twenty-one years doing things your way."

As the door closed behind her, Mike smiled. He knew how much Stacy liked getting in the last word. His anger had subsided, giving way to an all-out ache. The void he'd been desperately trying to cope with since leaving Stacy had just widened immeasurably. The painful throbbing in his arm from the gunshot wound was nothing in comparison to the painful throbbing in his heart. He loved her. And no fears, rantings, rationalizations or anything else he might try to come up with was going to temper that love.

Stacy's anger was just getting going as she stepped out of his room. The damn fool, Stacy muttered to herself. He gave a new meaning to the word "stubborn."

"So he yelled at you, too," Mrs. Gallotti said as she saw Stacy stomping down the hall. She had purposely waited in the small alcove lounge, guessing that her son would upset the girl. "Come, sit by me for a minute. Don't take it to heart. Didn't I tell you how stubborn that boy can be?"

"He's absolutely pigheaded," Stacy snapped, then realized that maybe putting Mike down was something Mrs. Gallotti thought only a mother could do. But Mike's mother grinned and nodded.

"I know, I know," she agreed. "What is there to

do?" She threw her hands up in the air.

"I'll tell you one thing," Stacy said, all at once breaking into a smile. "If I'd had a bowl of spaghetti handy in there, he would have had his second crowning."

They both laughed. Stacy felt better.

"You love him very much, yes?" Mrs. Gallotti's voice was no longer tinged with laughter.

Stacy sobered, too. "Very much."

"He's a hard man to live with," Mike's mother warned gently.

"He's a hard man to live without."

Mrs. Gallotti put her plump arm lovingly around Stacy. "I tell you what I think. I think my son has found himself a special prize—a blessing. He may be stubborn, my Michael. But he's no fool. I believe everything will come out good—you'll see. I know these things."

How could Stacy tell her that things weren't ever going to work out? That neither one of them could make the kind of commitment that Mrs. Gallotti believed would finally happen. How could she tell her that she was working hard to forget Michael Gallotti? Reflecting on her brief encounter with Mike, she understood that he, too, was working as hard as he could to forget her. She shouldn't have come today. But she had to.

Stacy gave Mike's mother a warm hug and kissed her gently on the cheek. If things had been different

—if she and Mike could have had different dreams
. . . Foolish thoughts, Stacy scolded herself as she
whispered a teary-eyed good-bye to this wise, dear
woman.

Seeing Mike again had been terrible for Stacy's
state of mind. Her anger had given way to worry,
concern, longing. Not that those feelings hadn't been
with her since he'd gone, but meeting him again had
magnified every one of them—most of all enlarging
her awareness of how much she loved him.

Joe had called a couple of days later, letting Stacy
know Mike was out of the hospital, and that he
would be home until the sling and bandages came off
next week. Stacy had blown up at Joe, accusing him
of playing cupid. What Mike did, where he was, and
where he went weren't any concern of hers, she told
him in no uncertain terms. She was not playing the
role of anyone's nursemaid. Joe had merely chuckled
and said, "So the guy's really gotten to you." Stacy
didn't bother to deny it. Everyone who knew her and
Mike could see the truth of their feelings for one
another, despite all the smoke screens they tried so
hard to erect. Sam and Annie had been on her back,
too. Sam especially kept telling her it was ridiculous
to view a loving relationship as interfering with the
creative process. He had used a few choice phrases
to bring home his point.

Stacy was tired of arguing with everyone. Only she

and Mike seemed to realize that there was no way they could ever work things out. On her part, she held up as proof of the impossibility of it all her inability to concentrate on her latest sculpture since she had seen Mike at the hospital.

One particular aspect of that meeting had disturbed her terribly. She did not like Mike seeing her as a controlling, manipulative woman. She understood that a certain amount of risk and danger were a necessary component of his work. All she had tried to do was make him realize that this assignment had seemed to become an obsession with him. Maybe he was out to prove a point, but in the process he might not live to see it proved.

She hated the thought of things ending on so angry a note. It gnawed at her constantly. Finally she realized she had to do something about it.

Stacy could practically feel Joe's broad grin over the telephone line even though he kept his voice carefully neutral when she asked for Mike's home address. Since it wasn't listed in the phone book, she'd had to decide between Joe and Mrs. Gallotti to find out where Mike lived. She chose Joe, figuring it wouldn't be fair to have Mike's mother make more of this than she should.

Mike lived in a nice Upper West Side neighborhood—nothing fancy, but pleasant. His place was in a small old brick building wedged between two large, modern rectangular apartment houses. His name was on the mailbox in the outer entry: 2C. She pressed the buzzer, and when Mike barked into the intercom, she identified herself. He didn't say anything. A moment later he buzzed her in.

Stacy walked up the stairs, not bothering with the elevator. She was tense and nervous, and her pulse was racing by the time she got to his floor. This little tête-à-tête could be worse than their last one. Why had she come here, anyway? But as soon as she saw Mike, who was standing by the open door, she knew exactly why.

He smiled—a bit hesitantly, Stacy decided—and she smiled back. When she stepped into his apartment, she was not surprised to see a sparsely decorated room, somewhat untidy, with few signs identifying the man who lived there. Mike, she thought, doesn't live in this place. He lives all over the world. This is merely where he rests and gets his second wind before starting out again. The apartment depressed her, but she tried to ignore her feeling, telling herself she wasn't discovering anything about Mike she didn't already know.

"As my mother would have said, you should have given me some warning. I'd have put on some homemade pasta and straightened up a bit." He slightly lifted his injured arm. "I do have a good excuse for the disorder, though." He gave her a wry grin.

"How's your arm feeling?" Stacy wasn't playing his game.

"Just fine and dandy," he announced, keeping up the glib style.

"Is that going to be your defensive maneuver this time? Keep it light, breezy. Or is this just for openers, and then we can go right into a fight and then I can storm out of here?"

"Stacy, you're always right in there hitting the bull's-eye. You shouldn't have come here."

He walked into the narrow galley kitchen. He had been struggling with a can opener and a tin of tuna for his lunch before Stacy showed up, and now, clumsily, he attacked the can again.

"Give it to me. I'll open it for you."

"I'm doing just fine, lady. I don't need any help. I thought that message had already gotten through loud and clear."

Stacy folded her arms across her chest and watched him continue to try to open the can with one hand. After a minute of getting nowhere, he looked over at her.

"Stop standing there looking so smug. Here, you win." He thrust the can opener in her direction.

Stacy took it from him and opened the can, while Mike stood beside her. She was acutely aware of the familiar scent of his aftershave lotion mingled with that subtle aroma of starch that professional laundries always use on shirts. Even more than the tangy aroma or his physical presence, she was struck with the powerful connection igniting between them—a fiery bond that nothing seemed to lessen.

Mike felt it, too. When she turned to him, she saw it in his eyes and in the tender smile on his lips. There was no fighting the desire that surged through them, no telling themselves that parting would be even harder this time. She stretched up her arms, encircled his neck and moved against him. Mike moaned, the pleasure of her pressed to him again more wonderful than ever.

"Oh, baby, I've missed you so much." He put his good arm around her and kissed her deeply.

"You taste so good," he whispered, trailing kisses down her neck and along the exquisite curve of her shoulder.

"Does this place of yours have a bedroom?" Stacy whispered breathlessly, willing to wrap herself around him anywhere.

He laughed in that sexy, provocative way she loved and took her by the hand, leading her through the living room to the bedroom.

Taking her in his arms again when they stepped inside, he slipped his hand under her jersey.

"I could use some help," he said sheepishly, lifting up the shirt. "I'm a lot better with two hands."

"I'll share mine with you anytime you want." She smiled, helping him undress her. It was a little more difficult getting Mike's clothes off, but they managed.

"We're a great team," he said, drawing her to him on the bed. Stacy picked up a hint of sadness in his tone.

This was not going to be a time for sorrow or regrets. They were two lovers given a moment's reprieve, and Stacy was determined to have that moment to its fullest.

"Make love to me, Mike. Make me feel like I'm soaring again to that magical place where only you and I exist. Let me touch you, kiss you, caress you. I want you so much." She began kissing him, skimming her lips down his chest. She felt him come alive with passion. When she returned to his lips, they were burning with desire.

Gently, careful not to hurt his injured arm, she began her rediscovery of his body. She wanted to recommit every part of him to memory. He felt even better than she had remembered in her attempts to keep him alive in her dreams and fantasies.

Mike, for all the awkwardness caused by his injured arm, made Stacy's body quiver with even greater desire than before. There was something added this time, a message they shared without words, a feeling that no matter what happened, they had something unique and indestructible linking them forever.

Together they reached that magical place—far more magical this time than either of them had remembered. They lay entwined in each other's arms for a long while after. There were no words to describe what they had experienced, no words to express what they felt for each other and nothing they could do about the pain that they knew would follow their parting.

Stacy lightly caressed his bandaged arm, a flagrant reminder of the dangers waiting for Mike. He took her hand in his.

"I'm going back to El Salvador on Saturday," he said softly.

"I knew you'd be leaving soon," she answered, resolved to accept reality.

He tipped her chin up and gazed at her. "I have news to cover there, but I've decided to hold off for now on that interview with the head of the rebel force."

"I'm glad." There was nothing more she could say. There would be other dangers, other risks. She was relieved he had finally decided to be sensible this time. She also hoped she had been part of the reason for his decision. But there would always be the next time. She forced herself to face another truth: Nothing had changed between them.

Mike caught hold of her arm as she began to get out of bed. She turned back to face him. His expression stunned her, there was such pain and passion there.

"I love you, Stacy." A tear rolled down his cheek. Stacy tenderly caught it on her fingertip.

"I love you too, Mike."

That part was simple, after all. And the rest—well, they both knew the sad ending. While admitting their love would make the parting harder, it would also allow them to face it with more honesty. There was no more hiding what they were each giving up.

Stacy quietly dressed and left the apartment. Neither of them said good-bye. It wasn't necessary to hear the words spoken. They rang loudly in their heads.

CHAPTER TEN

"What do you think, Zeke?" Stacy stood beside her model, eager for his reaction.

For a short while Zeke said nothing. He gazed at the monumental sculpture, then started to walk closer, finally circling it a couple of times. At last he looked back at her.

"Spectacular." His tone was almost reverential. "It is not only the best work you've ever done, but it is one of the most stirring, powerful sculptures I've seen, period."

"Thank you, Zeke." She finally let out her breath. She and Zeke had worked together for six months. He had been a fine model and, over time, a friend as well as someone Stacy respected. He had passed his law boards in the fall and he might easily have quit modeling then. But he stuck to his commitments and continued to model for Stacy right up to the end. He was a good man, and his praise meant a great deal to Stacy.

She was immersed in studying the nude sculpture, going over in her mind every line and curve. She hadn't fully absorbed the fact that it was truly finished, that tomorrow it would be picked up and transported to San Francisco. She was planning to follow the day after. The dedication of the nude wasn't for another week, but Stacy had decided to take some time off and have a little vacation in the San Francisco area. She felt Zeke's clear blue eyes watching her.

"You've got a great memory for detail, Stacy. You're still wrapped up in that newspaper man, aren't you?"

"Wrapped up" was an understatement. There was no hiding the depth of her feelings for Mike, the love as well as the pain that had grown more intense in these past six months. She hadn't been able to do anything about either problem. And working on this sculpture kept Mike constantly visible. With a wry smile, she squinted at Zeke. "It shows, huh?"

Zeke laughed loudly. "All sixteen feet of it, to be precise. I have a feeling you really didn't need me at all," he said, teasing, but there was more than a grain of truth in his observation.

"It isn't true, Zeke. You have been invaluable. Maybe in a way it's unfortunate for you that you share so many features with Mike. But believe me, that piece over there has a lot of you in it."

"Don't worry. Unlike some other models, I don't get hung up on that kind of thing. I was only joking." He paused for a moment, his eyes again drawn to the sculpture. "Actually, Stacy, I think this guy is universal. He is one man and he is all men. What is so fantastic about it is that he really does transcend the individual."

"That's why I entitled the piece *Fundamental Man.*" Stacy jabbed him lightly in the side. Her tone was teasing, but the truth was she felt deeply touched by Zeke's awareness of her accomplishment.

"I'm going to miss the guy," he said and grinned. "I don't think it's nice of you to move our old friend here off to the West Coast."

"I still wish you and Liz would come out for the dedication," she said earnestly. She did want Zeke and his wife to go. For the past few days, seeing the end of her work draw near, Stacy had been feeling sad and lonely. Those feelings had increased with each passing day, and now, as excited and pleased as she felt with her finished work, she also felt depressed. There was an empty, gnawing sensation in the pit of her stomach. Mike was in every ounce of that stone. She had put her heart and soul into that work, and Mike made up so much of both.

"You know how I feel about ceremonies," Zeke confided. "If I could have gotten out of all the rigmarole at my wedding, only making an appearance for the 'I do's,' I would have. Anyway, with Liz being over seven months pregnant, she's so grumpy you wouldn't want her around, either," he said with a laugh.

Stacy knew he was joking. He and Liz were exuberant about her pregnancy. For five months now Stacy had been hearing about almost nothing else. She was happy for them—and envious, too. Why was it that everyone else seemed to have such wonderful, loving relationships? Everyone but her. She kept telling herself that six months should have been enough time to get Mike Gallotti out of her system. All time had done was wedge him deeper into her heart.

After Zeke left, Stacy sat perched on a stool gazing at the nude sculpture. She had tried everything these past months to get Mike out of her mind. When she wasn't working she tried to fill all her idle moments by going out to any and every party, benefit, play and concert in town. She must have seen every single art show that had opened since Mike left. Her phone was always busy; there was always some eligible escort eager to take her out. But none of them ever made it to first base. Stacy tried to fool herself into believing that she was having a good time; that the social whirl of activity was helping to keep her thoughts of Mike at bay. But her dreams betrayed her, as did the sense of loneliness and desire that pursued her despite all her best efforts.

It also didn't help to have people like Zeke remind her how much her feelings showed and how unsuccessful she had been about getting Mike Gallotti out of her mind.

Her friend Sam had stopped nagging her about her adamant stance concerning love and art. But she frequently caught him looking at her with a kind of sad expression.

If she were going to be truthful, she would have admitted to Sam that he was right. She had finally realized that it wasn't loving someone passionately that interfered with her creative energy. It was having those feelings and not being able to give them expression that caused the real problem. What was the point of realizing or admitting that now? As Mike had said to her more times than she cared to remember, "Nothing has changed." For him, loving someone did interfere with his work. He wanted freedom without restrictions. At least Stacy had come to see that he wasn't so much afraid of her trying to tether him as he was of his own feelings of duty and obligation. Well, he was out there free as a bird. And obviously, Stacy thought with a mixture of anger and pain, he was perfectly content.

She hadn't heard one word from him since the day she left his apartment. It wasn't that she expected to. But she wanted to; she wanted to desperately. Going to the sculpture, she skimmed her palm along the cool stone. She had put so much of Mike in it. Now this was all she had of him. And even that would be gone tomorrow when the movers came to crate and transport the sculpture to San Francisco. Stacy

177

climbed the ladder, studying the rugged, earthy features of the stone face. She leaned over, placing a tender kiss on the cold, unyielding lips. Climbing down the ladder, she comforted herself as she had many times before with her fantasy of Mike reappearing when they were both old and gray. A foolish fairy tale, she chided herself. But she let herself contemplate it anyway.

"Would you like a newspaper or magazine, miss?" Stacy turned from the airplane window and looked up at the smiling flight attendant. The New York *Globe* was on top of the pile in the trim, attractive young woman's arms.

Okay, Stacy, she scolded herself, time to grow up and face reality.

"I'll take the *Globe*, thanks." Stacy took it gingerly from the woman's hand, placing it carefully on her lap. The first step hadn't been too difficult. Now she started arguing with herself. Why do I have to do this? Before Mike came careening into my life, I never paid much attention to the headlines. Arguments aside, she knew it was important now. The news of the day was not the issue, after all. It was coming to grips with the fact that Mike existed and was out there somewhere. Maybe reading his articles would make her face the reality of their separation. She hoped it might help.

There was no way to find out if it would have helped. She scanned the front page for his byline, then looked again more carefully. She began turning the pages, trying to find his name on each one. There was nothing there by him.

Stacy told herself that it wasn't unusual for a newsman, even one as famous as Mike, not to have something printed on a particular day. Still, it struck her as odd that the one time she decided to read the *Globe*, Mike's byline wasn't there. A wave of panic assaulted her. But she quickly reasoned that Joe would have let her know if anything had happened to Mike. Despite her ranting and raving about not giving a damn, she was well aware that Joe knew the truth.

Settling back in her seat, Stacy found the experience with the newspaper anticlimactic. She stared ahead at the movie screen in the front of the plane, watching the figures move about but not bothering to plug in her earphones. She did not feel up to concentrating on anything.

She closed her eyes after a while and tried to sleep, but when thoughts of Mike kept her awake, Stacy forced herself to focus on her plans for her five-day vacation. After the brief respite she would have to make an appearance at the dedication. Maybe she'd rent a car and go down along the coast to Big Sur, or head north to Napa Valley, tour the wineries and get tipsy on the samples. Smiling to herself, she decided the latter sounded more appealing just now. Anything to get her mind off Michael Gallotti.

* * *

Stacy swung her legs into the small sportscar. After four days in California she was still amazed at the sharp contrast in the weather from New York City: 65 balmy degrees on December fourth. She took a deep breath of the cool, lush air. It felt divine. Back home the normally gray city streets might even be covered with an even grayer, crusty coating of early snow. It only took moments for the white flakes to darken in New York.

She was glad she had come here several days before the dedication, giving herself her first real vacation in years. She had always told herself she was too busy to take time off. Actually she was afraid of lounging around, not working. The puritan ethic, Stacy said and laughed to herself. Maybe some of her father, a dyed-in-the-wool workaholic, had rubbed off on her after all. Mr. English could have retired from the family chemical company years ago. In fact, he had never needed to work in the first place. But the company was his life—that and squiring his wife around to all the right places, making sure they were both seen participating in all the right events. Stacy had accepted the fact years ago that her parents were snobs. Nice ones, but decidedly egotistical and ostentatious. It was in the fiber of their beings. She wondered for a moment what their reaction would have been to Mike. She had never told them anything about him. There had been no point. Stacy knew her mother had not given up hope that one of the choice eligible bachelors still running free in New York would wind up as her son-in-law. Stacy was certain her mother would not be fussy as long as his papers were in order and his blood was blue!

Her thoughts turned to Gina Gallotti, and Stacy realized she missed her almost as much as Mike. In short order Mike's mother had stolen Stacy's heart as surely as Mike had done. She missed her warmth and her joyful, positive approach to life. She could have used some of her wisdom and nurturing many times during these past few months. Whenever she felt the urge pressing in on her to call Mrs. Gallotti, she forced it down. It wasn't fair to his mother, and in the end it would be still more painful to Stacy.

The wineries did not lessen her ache as much as she had hoped. She loved the countryside and did tour a few of the more popular wine-producing houses, even sampling a good amount of the wine. All it seemed to do was make her feelings more acute, her thoughts more intense.

Driving the snappy rented sportscar through country lanes shaded by verdant, aromatic eucalyptus trees worked better. The wind whizzing against her face, the warmth, the tranquillity and the special beauty of this region were all soothing. As she drove she could let her mind go blank, allowing herself to relax for a while.

She stopped one night at a quiet inn in a picturesque town. After a light dinner, most of it left untouched, Stacy went to bed. Tomorrow she would have to be up early, as she was expected at the dedication by noon.

She remembered that last dedication. She could still picture Mike standing there, smiling at her wistfully and then, the next moment, vanishing into thin air, as if he had never existed. This time she would not have to worry about keeping her eyes away from his during the ceremony, she thought sorrowfully.

Tomorrow Mike would not be there. Again a wave of loneliness and sorrow overwhelmed her. Hugging herself tightly against the feeling of emptiness, she fiercely fought back the tears. In the end she gave in to her feelings and cried herself to sleep, convinced that nothing was ever going to lessen her pain.

"We can't tell you, Miss English, how excited we are about your sculpture. It's the perfect adjunct to the Center for Humane Studies—a bold statement of what we are all about." The director of the center held Stacy's hand as he spoke.

Stacy smiled warmly at the tall, attractive man. She could see that he was being sincere. When he held onto her hand a moment longer, she also could see that his enthusiasm had transferred from the sculpture to the sculptress.

Stacy gently extracted her hand. "Thank you, Dr. Adams—not only for your praise but for the lovely dedication itself. Sometimes these occasions can get overly elaborate. I much prefer a simple and to-the-point approach, which you've accomplished admirably." She smiled to herself, remembering the planning meeting for the *Peace and Harmony* sculpture and Derek's apoplectic responses to her demands. Inevitably, thoughts of Mike flashed through her mind as well. She shook her head clear of the thought, aware that Dr. Adams's eyes were still focused on her.

"I'd consider it an honor if you would have dinner with me tonight. It isn't often I get to take out a famous artist, and never one as beautiful as you."

"Thanks, Dr. Adams, but—"

"Before you come up with a no, first call me Tom, and second—reconsider." He smiled broadly. "It wasn't easy for me to get my nerve up, Stacy. I'm shy when it comes to celebrated women. You wouldn't want me to backslide now that I've finally forced myself to be so daring."

She knew he was pushing the truth, how much she wasn't certain. Tom Adams was a very successful and attractive man in his early forties. His sandy blond hair peppered with sprinklings of gray gave him just the right touch of distinction. There was an openness and charm about him that Stacy had to admit was appealing. Yet she hesitated about accepting.

She was given further time to consider Tom's invitation when a large, burly man came bustling over to her, his plump hand latching onto her arm.

"George Ealing, Miss English." He pumped her hand vigorously, still holding onto her arm with his other hand. Stacy took an immediate dislike to this youngish, unkempt man. She was always suspicious of people who sweated profusely when the weather did not warrant it. His name sounded vaguely familiar, but she couldn't place it until he added, "From the L.A. *Herald.*"

"Why yes, Mr. Ealing," Stacy said with a sharply condescending tone. "I recall reading one of your reviews awhile back."

He had the decency to flush for a moment. "I guess you weren't very pleased with that one." He laughed uncomfortably.

"Actually, Mr. Ealing, I found the review somewhat amusing. You must have been just starting out in the business at that point. In fact, my guess is that you were probably in the sports section or maybe movie reviews and had to fill in for the art critic."

Stacy enjoyed watching the flush growing steadily redder in Ealing's face. She certainly had no intention of giving him a hint of how upset that article had made her. When he mumbled something about this review being one she would appreciate, Stacy merely nodded disinterestedly. As she turned away she couldn't help thinking about the day she had seen Ealing's review. It was the same day that she and Mike had made love for the first time.

When Tom Adams came back over to her, she quickly thanked him again for his invitation to dinner but said she preferred to have an early dinner alone as she was returning to New York first thing in the morning.

Tom Adams knew when there was no point in arguing. Stacy may have appeared tentatively receptive a few minutes before, but now there was a cool, distant mask over her animated features. He nodded understandingly, but Stacy knew he couldn't begin to understand. Damn you, Mike, she cursed him silently, you've ruined me for any other man. None of them is you and you are all I want.

Her hotel was a few blocks from the center. After accepting congratulations from many others at the dedication and politely turning down several invitations, she managed to get away. She walked back to the hotel feeling drained. So many endings, she thought. Now that she had finished the sculpture and given it up, there was no longer anything tangible linking her to Mike. Only memories and dreams. Nothing that would satisfy her hunger or her ache.

The hotel was actually a gingerbread Victorian affair near the ocean. A large, homey porch wrapped around two of its sides, with wicker seats and rocking chairs scattered all about. Stacy had stayed here a couple of years ago and loved its quaint charm and stunning view of the sea. As she climbed the stairs to the porch she saw two rockers side by side, a sign on them and a yellow ribbon tying them together. Curious, she walked over to have a closer look. The sign said, Reserved.

"Will this spot do?"

Stacy whirled. Mike stood a foot away, holding two tall drinks in his hands. She was speechless.

"I hear that the sunsets from this porch are spectacular. And if you think it's easy to come by mint juleps in San Francisco, English . . ." He gave her one, but her hand was shaking so much she spilled some. He took her drink back and placed both glasses on the wide wood railing. His own hand trembled, Stacy realized as he set the drinks down.

"What are you doing here, Mike?" Her voice was a throaty whisper.

"What do you mean?" He grinned, stepping closer. "Wasn't this the plan—a pair of rockers, smashing sunsets, mint juleps . . ." He reached out and caressed her cheek, his hand still trembling.

"You don't look old and gray yet, Gallotti." She smiled back, her heart thumping to beat the band. Hold on, she told herself. You still don't know for sure what this is all supposed to mean.

"I may not be a lot older, English. But I'm a hell of a lot wiser." He slipped his hands onto her waist. "I realized that I want to spend the best years of my life with you, not my last ones. In fact, I don't want to waste one more moment."

He took her in his arms and kissed her. Light and playful at first, his kisses quickly grew passionate and urgent. Stacy clung to him, still afraid this was a delusion born of her longing. If she let go, he would surely vanish again. But his fierce, hungry embrace quickly convinced her. She could feel his body tremble, hear the words of love he whispered breathlessly in her ear. He was real, he was here. Stacy felt like she was going to burst with happiness.

Holding her in his arms, clinging to her with as much fervor as she clung to him, he was mindless of the tears streaming down his cheeks. He had almost lost her—almost lost the one person who really made life matter. He swore to himself that he would never let that happen to them again.

"Mike, I've missed you so much. I haven't stopped hurting for one moment since you left. But I still don't understand. You were so adamant about—about us."

"We both were, I thought." He understood her pain all too well. He had shared it every moment of their separation. But now the hurt had given way to a feeling of elation and joy. His still-moist eyes sparkled as he remembered how strongly he had believed loving meant being tied down. The light had finally dawned. Loving really meant freedom and the chance to have happiness and fulfillment. It took nothing away. It only gave.

Stacy smiled at him. She had almost forgotten that she had been as determined as Mike not to get deeply involved. Her determination had disappeared a long while ago.

"We are each impossibly stubborn," she said, her eyes shining through her tears. He looked so good, so incredibly good. She could hardly believe he was real. She still clung to him for dear life.

"I'm also mighty greedy," he whispered, releasing her just far enough to look down at her. "Memories just aren't as good as the real thing. And I want the real thing more than I ever thought possible." He cupped her chin. "I want all of you, Stacy English. I want to go to bed each night with you in my arms and wake up every morning to your grumpy frown." He grinned as she jabbed him playfully in the chest.

"I seem to remember one morning I wasn't very grumpy."

"I remember it too. Believe me, I remember." He kissed her parted lips, letting his tongue skim across them.

"You're right." She laughed joyfully. "You are greedy."

"Another one of my lousy traits." He laughed back. The laugh faded and he asked, "Can you cope with all of them?"

"A lot better than I've done coping without them, Mike." She placed her still-trembling hands on his cheeks. "Welcome home," she murmured, tipping his head down so that she could kiss him again. Then, tilting her head back slightly, she looked up into his warm hazel eyes. "But what about your work and being footloose and fancy free?"

He lifted her onto the railing with ease, so they were almost eye level. "You are now looking at the new managing editor of the International Desk."

"Joe's job?"

"Joe has been after me for the last two years to

take it over so that he could retire in peace. I always turned it down. I had my wild oats to sow." He grinned. "Now I've got more important oats to sow." he whispered, kissing the tip of her pert nose.

"Is this really what you want, Mike? Sitting behind a desk, giving out the exciting and dangerous assignments that you used to leap at . . ."

"What I really want is you. You and a family of our own. It's funny—for years I believed my dad was tied down to all of us, forced to settle for something he didn't really want. But you realized almost immediately what I've only just begun to understand. You assumed that my folks must have had a very special relationship. I can finally accept that they did. They really loved each other very much. I never fully appreciated that."

Stacy took his hand and squeezed it.

"I love you, Stacy. You are more important to me than scooting around the world. What do you think, babe? Are you still afraid that I'll use up all your creative energy if I hang around?" He'd asked the one unanswered question. It was the final missing link.

"Since we've been apart I've done some learning myself. I found out that loving doesn't hamper my creativity. It only adds to it. I think it's what's been missing from my work for so long—that special quality that is finally there. The sculpture of the nude is the best thing I've ever done, Mike—because it was created out of love."

"We do have a remarkable ability, English, to always be on the same wavelength," he said, hugging her to him. Then he slid his hands down her arms and took hold of her wrists. "I haven't gone down to the center to see the sculpture yet. I wanted to go with you alone, once the crowds from the dedication went away."

Hand in hand they walked back to the center. Stacy stood in front of Mike, his hands lightly squeezing her shoulders as he pressed her against him while they both looked up at the awesome sculpture. Stacy turned her head toward him to see the look of pride and pleasure in his eyes.

"I always did want to be immortalized. I just had to find the right woman to make my dream come true." He turned her around to face him. "To make all my dreams come true." Embracing her, he gazed up again at the statue. "Thanks, buddy," he whispered to the stone giant.

A middle-aged couple walked by. The woman looked up at the sculpture and then over at Mike, who stood so near it.

Poking her husband, she said in a voice loud enough for Mike and Stacy to hear, "Will you look at that, George? That fellow over there looks just like he could have modeled for that naked statue."

"Quite a coincidence, Mildred. But it's not too likely." He chuckled.

Mike caught Stacy up in his arms and they both

laughed. "Yes, sir, quite a coincidence. Really amazing when you think about it," said Mike.

"Wonderfully amazing," Stacy concurred, pulling him toward her. "A remarkable resemblance," she murmured, kissing him tenderly, "but I'll take the model over cold stone anytime."

LOOK FOR NEXT MONTH'S
CANDLELIGHT ECSTASY ROMANCES ®: